RED GOLD

Sandy Nadeau

I0610445

This is a work of fiction. Names, characters, places, and incidents either are the product of the author's imagination or are used fictitiously, and any resemblance to actual persons living or dead, business establishments, events, or locales, is entirely coincidental.

RED GOLD

COPYRIGHT 2013 by SANDY NADEAU

Contact Information: titleadmin@pelicanbookgroup.com

All scripture quotations, unless otherwise indicated, are taken from the Holy Bible, New International Version[R], NIV[R], Copyright 1973, 1978, 1984 by Biblica, Inc.™ Used by permission of Zondervan. All rights reserved worldwide. www.zondervan.com

Cover Art by *Nicola Martinez*

Harbourlight Books, a division of Pelican Ventures, LLC
www.pelicanbookgroup.com PO Box 1738 *Aztec, NM * 87410

Harbourlight Books sail and mast logo is a trademark of Pelican Ventures, LLC

Publishing History
First Harbourlight Edition, 2014
Paperback Edition ISBN 978-1-61116-322-3
Electronic Edition ISBN 978-1-61116-321-6
Published in the United States of America

Dedication

I want to thank Jesus, who gave me a desire to share stories long ago and provides more adventures in my life. Without His guidance, this dream of mine would not be as fulfilling. To my daughter Trisha, who helped me so much in the beginning creation of this story, who cheers me on endlessly, and relentlessly. You are my Sunshine. To my loving husband, Ron. For all the years of putting up with my dream and drying the tears. It's official honey! I love you. And my parents, Norb and Dorothy, for always encouraging me to persevere.

A special thanks to Nicola for giving me a chance three different times, then accepting this story. For the wonderful edits from Nicola and Jamie. I learned so much through this process. Thank you both!

May all who travel the back country of Colorado, love it as much as I do.

And Jesus said to him, "I am the Way, and the Truth, and the Life; no one comes to the Father, but by Me."
(John 14:6)

1

The stench of burning brush assaulted her.

No! Mandy ran for the porch, grabbed the wand of the triangle suspended from the roof, and clanged the warning. Dread and panic crept up. Her heart raced.

Smoke billowed over the ridge. She knew flames inched towards the dry brush that lay between them and the guest ranch.

"Jon!" Mandy screamed for her husband as she clanged the triangle, and then dashed into the house.

The screen door slammed shut.

"Jon!" She grabbed the phone and ran back outside to the triangle. Visions of losing everything rose in her mind.

Barney, their black and brown Australian Shepherd, stood outside the door flinging himself into the air and barking frantically.

"What's going on?" Jon's thundering steps came from the house.

She dialed 911 and clanged the triangle while waiting for the operator to answer. "Fire!" she yelled to Jon. "There's smoke coming up from over the ridge to the south." Beads of sweat ran down her forehead.

"What's your emergency?" The dispatcher's voice came over the phone.

Mandy stopped clanging. "Fire to the south of High Country Safaris off County Road Five. Hurry!"

Jon sailed past her, not even touching the porch

steps.

Ranch hands ran from the barn and the bunkhouse, some men still pulling on boots.

Mandy pointed to the smoke rising over the ridge.

"I see it, Miss Mandy," Mike hollered. His boots stirred up a cloud of dust as he changed direction. "I'll get the water truck." He ran towards the garage with George, another ranch hand, on his heels.

Mike and George hopped in the passenger seat. They tore up the service road towards the rising smoke.

The others grabbed shovels, picks, and axes.

Mandy threw the phone onto the porch chair and headed to her old Willy's Jeep.

Barney jumped off the porch ahead of her and ran in circles.

She pointed a warning finger at his spot under a tree near the porch. "Go lay down, Barney. You stay! I mean it."

Barney whined, sat back down, but his front paws bounced side to side. He obeyed, but panted heavily and watched after the crew going into the smoke. The dog let out an occasional bark as she left.

"Lord, please, stop this fire... please."

A blaze could take off, especially after such a dry winter and all the dead trees from the beetle infestation. Spring rains had been sparse in the mountains of Colorado, and the sun was hot at their 7,900 foot elevation.

The vehicle bounced off every rock and pothole in the old dirt road, but she didn't care about the jarring her body endured. Her knuckles grew white as she gripped the steering wheel.

Over the ridge, Jon and the hands were flanking

the fire.

A deep chill ran up her spine, and her palms went cold.

Shovels and pick axes flew up and down with rhythmic movement as the men worked to throw dirt onto the crawling flames.

She scanned the potential route of the fire. It wasn't that large, maybe over an acre, but as the wind picked up, it would only get worse. If the fire made it into the trees, there would be no way to stop the flames before they finished off the forest. And their ranch.

Mandy pulled to a stop next to the other vehicles.

Mike had parked the water truck close and was hauling the hose towards the flames.

She got out, found a shovel and ran. "Where do you want me?" She screamed over the motor on the water truck. Smoke drifted into her nostrils. Her eyes watered. The acrid smell caused her nose to scrunch up.

"Right flank," Jon yelled back.

Mandy went to the end of the line and began to shovel away pine needles and other debris to get to the dirt to throw on the flames.

The fire had crawled its way through the dry winter remains at a steady rate. They had to get a line cut around the front.

Mike sprayed water as a couple guys dug into the earth, revealing more embers, trying to get a handle on the battle.

"How could this have started?" Mandy's words huffed out with shortened breaths.

Sirens blared in the distance. Minutes later the first of the fire department's grass-fire trucks made their way to the scene. Three men jumped out, grabbed their portable water tanks, and started spraying the edges of the fire. Smoke thickened and grew whiter as the water collided with the flames.

Mandy backed away as firefighters with two more vehicles arrived, her muscles screaming from the sudden exertion and fear.

The crew got the fire surrounded and continued to work the hot spots until they were sure it would finish dying out.

All the ranch hands who manned the shovels and picks took a step back, leaning heavily against their tools and gasping in the smoke-filled air.

Blackened earth smoldered below the tall ponderosa pines.

Mandy joined Jon as he walked over to Chief Radner.

"Glad you got here so fast, Pete," Jon said.

"Good thing you guys got after it so quickly. It's real lucky this didn't take off any further than it did. We'll take care of the mop up. I'll post a couple of the guys to watch for any hot spots for a couple of hours. We can't trust anything with as dry as we've been."

"It's not been a good spring, that's for sure. Thanks, Pete." Jon wiped his forearm across his forehead.

"That was close." Mandy looked at her watch. "Jon, oh no...we're going to be late for the meeting with the county."

He checked his own watch. "We've got to go." He thanked the crew with a wave as he and Mandy ran for the vehicle.

They would still have to stop at the house for his briefcase. They had to have the paperwork.

Her heart rate ramped up in the panic of missing

this vital appointment. Sweat ran down her spine. "We're never going to make it in time, Jon, and look at us. We're a mess. Shonee will get the upper hand if we miss this meeting. He'll say anything without us there."

"Let's not assume the worst about him. We just have to get there and explain what happened." His reassurance did nothing for her.

They raced on the back roads into town.

Mandy grabbed the cleansing wipes in the glove box and tended to the smudges they both wore on their faces, hands, and arms. If she didn't do something, her anxiety would get the best of her. "Lord, get us there in time, please." Her foot tapped out the words and her angst.

They arrived at the county courthouse.

Twelve minutes after ten. "Oh, Jon, we're so late." She slammed the door.

Jon grabbed her hand, and they ran up the granite steps of the courthouse. They rushed down the hall and rounded the corner only to bump into Mr. Shonee.

"Well, look who finally showed up." Mr. Shonee's face held a gruff but satisfied sneer. The short, white-haired man leaned against his cane. "You can quit yer runnin'. I let the court know that you obviously don't trouble yourselves enough to follow up on the cares and concerns of your neighbors. Your project is dead. You won't be building up near the mine, and I won't have to listen to it or watch all those rotten brats play near my property. You might as well sell that side back to me." He stared at them.

"There was a fire. You should be glad we stopped it. If we hadn't seen it, it could have spread to your property." Mandy panted out the words. She bent over, placing her hands on her knees to catch her breath.

"A fire. That's a handy excuse." Mr. Shonee growled, and then hobbled towards the door dependent on his cane.

Mandy straightened and turned.

Jon grabbed her arm to prevent her from going after the man. "Don't say anything that will make this worse than it is. Let's go see if we can talk to the judge."

Mandy growled under her breath and followed her husband. There were some very un-Christian things she wanted to say.

They found the right office and requested a moment of the judge's time from the receptionist seated at a desk.

"I'm sorry Mr. and Mrs. Phillips. Judge Markum is in court now."

"We had a fire on the property. There was no way to make it in time. Surely we can have a minute to talk to him," Mandy blurted.

"The judge has ordered a stop on your project. I'm really sorry. He needed to hear your side of this for you to continue."

Jon's jaw tightened as he stared at the woman. "The fire was circumstances beyond our control. We need to see him."

"I'll let him know what happened, but we will have to call you and set up another time. Our schedule is tight, so it may take a few weeks before we have an opening. For now, you just have to keep your project on hold. I'm very sorry."

"But..." Mandy knew it wouldn't do any good to discuss it with the woman.

Jon thanked the receptionist and put his arm around his wife as they turned to leave.

Mandy squeezed her now aching forehead.

"Let's get back to the ranch." Jon turned to the woman. "Please let us know as soon as possible when we can meet with Judge Markum."

"Of all the worst timing. Why a fire this morning...why a fire at all?" She slapped at the soot and dust on her jeans as if she could erase the fire scene.

"Let's just be thankful we caught it before it did any real damage. We'll just have to deal with this another time. We've got to get ready for the guests coming in on Sunday afternoon."

Fifteen minutes later, they turned into the driveway of High Country Safaris.

Chief Radner sat in his truck with the door open scratching Barney's ears.

Barney's whole backside wiggled as he waited for them. The dog's antics barely brought a smile to Mandy's lips.

"Surprised you're still here Pete. Is everything all right up there?" Jon asked.

Barney circled them and sat, leaning against Mandy's leg.

The chief showed little emotion. "Jon, Mandy...looks like the fire was deliberate. We definitely found traces of an accelerant and tracks in the dirt. We are listing this as suspicious while we investigate further."

"Deliberate? Well, we can sure guess who's behind that. Shonee made sure we couldn't show up this morning."

"Mandy, let's not rush into accusations." Jon put

his arm around her.

She pulled away, arms flailing, which caused Barney to lose his footing. "Jon, you know as well as I that Shonee would do anything to make life miserable for us. He always has and always will." Mandy paced in a tight pattern slapping her hand against her thigh

"I thought about him, too," Chief Radner said. "I know he tends to be a pain for you guys. We'll be talking to him. Don't worry about that. For now, at least the fire is out. We'll take care of the rest." Pete shook hands with Jon, gave Mandy a hug, got in his truck and drove away.

"Well." Jon blew out a breath. "Not much we can do now. We might as well put our energy into getting ready for the guests. How many do we have coming in this week?"

"We have six cabins reserved. I'll go see if the cleaning crew is here. I have to get busy right now or I'll lose it."

"I'll check on the cars and make sure the tune-ups have been done." Jon turned and headed to the lined up four-wheel drive vehicles.

"Jon?"

"Yeah, hon?"

"Will this work out? We've had such exciting plans this winter. I really wanted to get the town site built this summer for the kids." She leaned against the porch post and kicked at the gravel of the parking area.

Jon walked back and pulled her into his arms. "We just have to be patient, Mandy. We have to trust Him and wait for His timing. I'm disappointed too, but I believe our plans will happen. In His time. I still believe the ideas came from up above, so we'll be faithful. Our guests will get to enjoy our plan.

Eventually."

"You know it's not my strong suit. Waiting, and the dreaded 'P' word. I'm not a patient woman."

"You're not?" Jon hugged her a moment longer. He stepped back, put his hand on her cheek. "I love you, Mandy."

"I love you, too."

2

Mandy paused at the door of the cafeteria as Allie, the head of housekeeping for High Country Safaris, gave instructions to the teens they'd hired from church for the season.

Mandy feigned a cheery face as she entered. "Hi everyone. How are you all?"

A collective "Hi, Miss Mandy," resounded. About ten teens were on staff this summer. Many of them were able to get credit at school for starting a job early. It always turned out to be a blessing for everyone.

Mandy loved building relationships with these teenagers. She missed when her kids were that age, so it helped to have the teens every summer. Her and Jon's own grown children attended college, their daughter in California, their son in Chicago. She didn't like being so far away from them, but she knew God wanted them there, and now she could fill her life with even more young people.

Allie looked back at the teens. "OK, you've got your assignments. Get to work."

Chairs scraped against the floor. The animated, collective voices soon over-powered all other noise.

Allie pulled out a chair and pointed for Mandy to sit. "I talked to Pete when I got in this morning. Is everything all right? You don't look good."

"Thanks a bunch."

"You know what I mean. Sit, spill it."

Mandy plopped into the chair, leaned her elbow

on the table, and rested her chin in the palm of her hand. "The fire made us late for the meeting with the county. Shonee sabotaged us with the judge. We missed him by minutes before he headed into court. His secretary has to set up a new appointment, but since we were late, I don't imagine they'll be in too much of a hurry. I'm so frustrated. Did Pete tell you he found signs of an accelerant? Someone was up there. Someone set it. Shonee has to be involved. He's fought all our efforts to improve the ranch. There's no other person who would want to hurt us. I don't know why that man has to cause us so many problems." She slammed her fist on the table. "I know it isn't very Christian of me, but I can't stand him. I wish he'd move away."

"Calm down. I know. It's hard to be gracious to someone who causes endless trouble and heartache. We just have to keep doing what we do. If the Lord wants the ranch to have the old west mini-town site, it will happen. We have a mission here to provide a great adventure to our guests and minister the love of God to them as well. Come on. Let's help Sue with the registrations and finish planning the trips. You'll feel better being busy."

"You sound like Jon. But you're right. I need to get to work and forget about what happened this morning. I can't do anything about it right now, anyway." Mandy shook her head at her own attitude towards the man. A heavy sigh escaped as she asked for forgiveness in her heart.

The women headed to the office located in the corner of the building. The knotty pine paneling offered warmth to the room. Sunlight poured through the large window that faced south where Sue sat at her desk already hard at work. She had run the office for two years now, freeing Mandy up to do other things.

"Hey, Sue. We thought we'd give you a hand on guest preps."

"Hi, ladies. Great. I can always use the help. I heard about the trouble this morning."

"We missed the meeting with the judge because of the fire."

"Oh, no. Interesting it would happen when you had an appointment concerning the area. Makes you wonder. I'm just going over the registrations. We still need to match the Jeeps to the type of outing the guests signed up for."

Since one side of their property backed up to the National Forest, the four-wheeling trails were endless. With it being springtime, the high country would have a lot of waterfalls. Not as dramatic as when it followed a heavy winter, but none the less beautiful. The wildflowers would just be starting to bloom.

"I'll set up the route options for those taking the Jeeps out on their own. Looks like only a few will be taking the guided tours."

Allie took note of the cabins reserved for the week so she could keep fresh linens available.

Sue's eyebrows went up. "Only two groups requested the ghost town routes this week. I guess people are still getting over cabin fever and want to see the open spaces instead of focusing on the hidden treasures in the back country."

"I can't blame them. I'm ready for some vista views myself. It may have been a drier winter this year, but it lasted too long." Mandy answered. "I miss it when Jon and I can't get into the back country and explore."

"OK, so we have two groups for ghost towns." Allie said. "Hand me the history booklets for those locations. Do we have the welcome packets ready?"

Sue pointed. "The bags are over on the shelf. The kids did a good job."

Allie turned towards the shelf. "I checked the storeroom earlier. We do need to order more energy bars soon. But we have enough for another month of guests."

"Oh Mandy, Tommy was in earlier. One of the Jeeps was having some kind of problem. I sent Jon over to talk to him about it."

"I'm heading over there in a bit. Thanks."

ஃ௦ஷ

After lunch, Mandy went to the garages to check in with Jon. She would also check on the horses. There were only two vehicles left in the six bay garage. Tommy's legs stuck out from under one of them.

Jon squatted next to him with a wrench in his hand.

Mandy put her hands on Jon's shoulders giving him a little neck rub. He leaned into her.

"How's it going, Tommy?" Mandy shouted over the blaring Country-Western tune on the radio and the clanking of wrenches.

"Hey, Miss Mandy." Tommy rolled out from under the vehicle sitting up as his head cleared the undercarriage. He grabbed the rag stuffed in his pocket and wiped his hands. "It's goin' good. Found a leak in one of the lines. Don't quite get that. There's never leaks in my vehicles. Runnin' good now, but I'm not braggin'." He flashed his toothy grin.

Mandy chuckled.

Jon winked at her.

Tommy's pride in vehicle care ranked higher than any of the mechanics.

"Good job, Tommy. Keep it up. If you two haven't eaten, you better head in there soon or they'll put the food away." She left to walk around the property and check on the appearance of the grounds. The wranglers had brought the horses in from the pasture last week. They were groomed and ready to ride.

Barney fell into step next to her.

"Hey, buddy. You staying out of trouble?" She scratched his ears and stared around. The property was cleaned of all the winter debris. Her gaze moved up in the direction of the fire. She stared at what she could not see.

The afternoon sun warmed everything it touched. She closed her eyes and turned her face upward to take in a good dose of vitamin D.

Barney leaned against her leg, panting.

After a couple of minutes, long, strong arms enveloped her.

She leaned her head back until it rested on Jon's shoulder, "Mmm. This is what I needed. Isn't it wonderful out today?"

"How do I never surprise you?" he whispered in her ear.

"Because you belong here. Your arms are supposed to be around me. At all times."

"I'll have a hard time getting my work done, then."

"Get someone else to do it."

Jon chuckled. "Yeah, right. I do need to talk to you. Can we go sit?"

Mandy turned and looked into his eyes. "I know that look. Do I want to know?"

"Just an update on the fire. I sent Nate and Mike back up to look around. There's something else, too."

"Well, let's go to the porch swing and talk. Want some lemonade?"

"Definitely."

Mandy went in and filled a couple glasses with the fresh lemonade she'd made last night. She backed out the squeaking screen door, and let it shut with a bang.

Jon reached out for the glass and smiled.

"What are you grinning about?"

"I just like lookin' at you."

Mandy sat next to him and slapped his leg. "Oh stop. Now what did Nate tell you?"

"I had them look around the area for any other clues. You know, the fire almost got up to the level area where we want to build the play town outside the mine entrance. If it had caught enough wind, it would have devastated the area. As it is, we'll have to do a lot of grooming to hide the damage. Some more plantings. I think an aspen grove would look good in there. Anyway, Nate realized something while up there."

"What?"

Jon took her hand. "There were footprints around the area. Even up by the mine opening. It looks like the tracks took off fast. Do you know if any of the staff had any reason to be up there?"

"Not that I know of. We don't allow anyone up there right now, anyway. For one thing, we're all too busy to be near the mine, but most important, it isn't safe until we can get someone in there to shore up the walls. Is the entrance still closed off?"

"It is, but not as well as it could be. We might have

to get a solid door welded against the opening instead of the fencing we have in place. It's too easy to slip past there if someone wanted to. I'll take some of the guys up there and check around some more. I want to look inside the cave just to be sure. "

"OK, but be careful. Until we get the inspectors in there, the mine will always make me nervous. I can't wait until we get it all taken care of. Was there something else?"

"Uh...yeah. Tommy didn't tell you exactly what he found." Jon looked off towards the garage.

Mandy set her glass on the side table. "Jon, what's going on?

"There wasn't just a leak. Once Tommy got under there, the brake line had a clean cut in it. Not something that could just happen."

"What are you saying?"

"I don't know. It just bothers me. You know how well he takes care of things. It doesn't make sense."

"I don't understand what's going on around here."

3

"I'm so glad our church has an early service so none of us have to miss it." Mandy and Jon led the caravan of vehicles back to the ranch.

Excitement filled the air for the startup of the summer activities.

She smiled as she looked out the window at the perfect Colorado day of sunshine, blue skies, and a very comfortable seventy degrees.

After a quick lunch, everyone went into "last-minute-check" mode of their particular area. The cars started to arrive.

Jon and Mandy stood on the porch waiting for the guests.

"Ready to welcome everyone?" Jon smiled.

"Can't wait." Mandy grinned right back.

Barney sat at their feet.

The vehicle pulled up to the office. Three young boys bounded out of the car with their cowboy hats and sunglasses already in place. The youngest ran towards the corral screaming all the way. The other two boys ran after him.

Barney joined in the run to the corrals.

"Boys, don't go far," the man yelled in their direction.

"Welcome to High Country Safaris." Jon walked towards the man extending his hand.

"Come on in," Mandy added with a wave. "Don't worry about the boys. They'll be fine. Our wrangler is down at the corral. He'll watch over them. We'll get you all settled in for your adventure."

"We're the Reynolds family. We sure have been looking forward to this. It's beautiful up here," the man said.

"You haven't seen anything yet. Wait until we get you up in the back country, you won't believe it." Jon led Mr. Reynolds into the office to do the necessary paperwork.

Mrs. Reynolds opted to stay on the porch so she could still see her boys. "We live east of Denver, where it's flat. We've wanted to do a real mountain trip for a long time. We haven't since the boys were born, but they're older now so it's easier. We were really excited after seeing your website and all that you have to offer."

"Well, we're glad you came and can't wait for you to see everything." Mandy replied. "I saw that you signed up for a Jeep tour. We'll get Randy, one of our guides, to take you to see some amazing sights. The wild flowers are just starting to come up at this elevation, so I hope you have lots of memory in your camera."

"We brought a few camera chips. I'm glad the kids get out of school so early so we can do a trip like this before the summer gets too busy. The boys have been so excited to go fishing."

"Oh, good. We have equipment and the pond is all stocked and ready. It's our private pond, so no limits and no license required. If they catch any, you are welcome to fix them for dinner, or if you'd rather we can probably convince one of our cooks to grill them up for you."

"Wonderful." The woman wrinkled her nose. "I'm

not much for cleaning fish."

Rosie, one of their teen helpers, arrived after a call on the two-way radio. The Reynolds family followed their guide to a two-bedroom cabin. As she led the way, Rosie gave them the Ranch's fire safety procedure and tidbits of information about the area.

Mandy watched from the porch as the family admired their living quarters' decor. A carved wooden bear holding a welcome sign was on the first step. The buildings sported either a moose, elk, fish, or bear theme. One room had a queen-sized bed and the second room had bunk beds. All the cabins had kitchenettes.

As the day went on, guests were checked in and settled.

As Jon did the paperwork, Mandy guided various children to the pond and corrals, and handed out brochures and extra towels when requested.

Mandy and Jon let everyone spend this first day getting to know the grounds, check out the horses, take a short walk to the fishing pond, or just relax on the porches and barbeque their dinner. Guests could always go to the cafeteria if they didn't feel like preparing their own food.

As the last of the people followed their guide to the final cabin, Mandy sighed.

"Good start to the season," Jon commented, as she walked up on the porch.

"Except for the fire." Mandy was pensive, still a little worried even as a slight, wet burnt smell lingered in the air when the breeze came out of the south.

❧

Twilight crept in, and the sunset colored the sky between the tall pine trees.

After dinner, various guests had wandered around for a bit, but now, as stars popped out in the dark sky, everyone in camp settled down for the night.

Mandy flipped on the overhead light in their bedroom, looking around at the sage green walls decorated with pine-cone trimmed wallpaper. The soft colors never failed to calm her. Jon came in from doing his nightly routine check of the barn, the garages, and walking around the camp to make sure all was well.

Barney curled up on his bed in the corner, after circling several times.

"Any conclusions up at the mine? I never got a chance to ask." Mandy changed into her blue silk pajamas.

Jon pulled his shirt over his head. "No, not really. I went up with Nate, Phil, and George. We saw the tracks and followed them, but they stopped after a few feet. We checked the fencing across the entrance, which seemed secure. We looked inside the mine with the flashlights and really didn't notice anything different.

"I just can't imagine what anyone could be up to. Even if the same person had anything to do with the fire, what reason could they have to snoop around? The mine played out decades ago. There's nothing up there, and it's on our private property."

"I know Shonee never likes anything to change, but this is ridiculous to try and stop us from building a little town for the kids. It's barely even visible from his property. Somebody else has to be behind this."

"Yeah, but who?"

Mandy turned on her small lamp by the bed while Jon shut off the main light. They crawled under the covers. Jon rolled over, wrapped his arms around his wife, and pulled her close. She loved this time of day.

Jon kissed her forehead. "Well, whoever it is, I don't think we'll have any trouble now with so many people around. Let's just focus on giving everyone a great week of adventure. But just to make sure, we better put some prayer over it all."

They both closed their eyes, and Jon led a prayer of thanks and for protection over everyone. He added a request that they have an opportunity to witness to their guests during their stay at the ranch. Then he prayed for his wife's strength to do all the work she had ahead of her.

Mandy sighed and smiled as they both closed with "Amen."

Jon kissed her again and rolled over.

Their nightly routine was as much a part of their lives as the guests who came every summer.

Mandy grabbed a book from the nightstand to read a chapter or two before she gave in to sleep.

4

In the morning, one of their guides came down with a migraine.

Mandy stepped in to take over the tour. She loved any excuse to be out of the office. Her charges were a family of three: Dad, Mom, and their thirteen-year-old daughter, who appeared quite unhappy with their plan for the day. The girl's face held no expression, her gaze locked mostly on her pink tennis shoes, her arms crossed tight over her chest. The parents, however, had looks of optimistic excitement.

The sunny skies were a good sign.

Mandy extended her hand in greeting. "Good morning. How are you all today? Are you ready for some back country adventure?"

"We sure are, aren't we, Jenny?"

A scowl was the only answer.

The father cleared his throat. "I'm Rick Carter, and this is my wife, Connie. The happy one is our daughter, Jenny."

Another scowl from the girl.

"Show us some sights." Rick smiled.

"You're going to enjoy it up there. I love taking new folks out into the back country." Mandy loaded a basket into the back of the red Jeep.

Once everyone buckled in, Mandy headed up the dirt road to the northwest. "Did you get some sun block on? There's some in your welcome pack and you'll need it at this altitude. With the top off the Jeep, ears and shoulders are targets. Be sure you drink a lot of water, too. I brought plenty. It helps ward off altitude sickness that can give you a nasty headache. Would you like a tour of the old ghost town up on the pass? It's a good example of life in a mining town in the 1800's."

"That sounds great." Rick reached for the tube of sunscreen his wife handed to him.

As they bounced along the dirt road, Mandy pointed out various plants. The ponderosa pines stood majestically along the roadside and up the hills. Kinnickinick covered the forest floor with its deep green, succulent leaves. Paintbrush flowers had just started to reach up from the ground with their red bushy tops ready to spring open. Pine needles and pine cones stuck up out of the mix everywhere. Many of the trees had the tell-tale rusty red needles.

"Why are the needles red on some of the trees?" Connie asked.

"Colorado's been suffering from a pine beetle infestation across the state which is affecting the lodge pole pines. The tiny beetles infected with a fungus bore into the bark." She slowed the vehicle and pointed to a particular tree near the road. "You can see the pitch tubes oozing out of the bark where the beetles had entered. They lay their eggs, and the larvae feast on the tree. The fungus actually kills the tree. When the larvae are grown, they fly off and the same cycle happens to the next tree. "

"Gross." Jenny said from her slouched position in the back seat.

"Yeah, it is gross. It's gross how we are losing our forests to such a little bug. Our ponderosa pines are getting hit by the Ips beetle and a lot of those are being lost."

Rick scowled. "Can't they do anything to stop it?"

"No, not really. Sprays can be a deterrent, but they don't necessarily kill the bugs. They're very prolific. If we don't cut the trees down, the bug problem escalates. As you can see by just this area here, that task would be daunting. It is hard to keep ahead of the little buggers. The problem reaches from Mexico to Canada. We are losing thousands upon thousands of acres of forest."

"What a shame." Connie eyed the woods.

"Yes, it is, but the trees are cycling through. This has actually happened several times over the last five hundred years. It'll be a very different landscape in five to ten years. But, the Lord will work it out."

Mandy couldn't help but catch the raised eyebrows reflecting in her mirrors.

When they reached the crest of the hill, another road, smaller in width, led off to the right. The Jeep bounced through the turn and the forest grew thicker.

"We are actually now on Forest Service land. It's isolated back here so not too many people find this area. Which is good, because the old buildings you are about to see have survived fairly well."

Mandy made another turn onto what barely resembled a road. The Jeep bounced over some rocks and headed into a more open area. The passengers held on to the framework above their heads. Checking in her mirror, Mandy saw that Jenny still had her arms crossed and was slouched down, letting the jolting shake her up. Mandy could feel the girl's knees in the back of her seat.

The gray remains of old buildings stood before them.

Mandy caught the barest glimmer of wide-eyed wonder in Jenny's eyes. "Welcome to Sugar Creek."

"Wow. How old is this place?" Rick asked.

They walked over to the nearest structure with its weather-worn wood and rusty, odd shaped nails.

"We're not really sure, but some of the historical records indicate around 1875. Prospectors discovered this area when they saw good color, which meant gold. When the word got out, people flocked in and were disappointed in a short amount of time. They found some gold, but it played out fast. This town may have had around fifty people in its prime."

"Isn't it interesting that people would live way up here, Jenny?" Connie asked her daughter.

"Seems pretty dumb to me. There wouldn't be anything to do."

"Oh, there'd be plenty. They worked hard in those days just to stay alive. They had to hunt for food every day. You can't grow much at this altitude so it took a lot of preparation to be ready for winter. And they always had to be on the lookout for mountain lions or rogue bears."

"Mountain lions!" Jenny jumped out from a crooked old doorway, eyes wide.

"Sure. They're the residents of the mountains. Don't worry, with this many together, they won't bother us. Just don't wander off alone, and never, ever run if you see one. They'll think you are prey and catch you faster than you can blink."

Jenny scooted closer to her father.

"A man by the name of Obadiah Gilman arrived here with the prospectors. He soon found out how hard he had to work to find gold, but saw more and more people arrive or pass through every day. He decided to open up a trading post to serve the needs of the new residents." Mandy walked over to one of the buildings at the center of the settlement.

"This is believed to be the store, because of its size. Come on over. You'll see what's left of a large counter. Mountain men could bring their pelts and barter for more provisions to take back up into the hills to keep prospecting. Old Obadiah became more and more greedy as the mining diminished and some people moved away. The residents who remained knew he was cheating them out of their hard-earned income. When the community found proof, an angry mob chased Obadiah out of town. Not too long after that, the town died."

"Wow. That's quite a story." Rick commented.

"We've collected many of these stories in the history booklets in the office. Our history is so important."

Jenny made a grunting sound. "What good is history? It doesn't matter anymore."

"Sure it does. It tells so much of where we've been, what people had to go through to get us where we are today. It helps us appreciate what we have."

Jenny rolled her eyes.

"I find it fascinating." Connie stood looking over every building.

They explored the town site a bit more, Jenny sticking close as she gazed in every direction. Her feet slipped on the gravel paths, but her arms stayed wrapped tight around her.

The rest of the morning was spent looking at amazing vistas of the mountain ranges from the old Jeep roads. The highest peaks in the distance still wore a covering of bright white snow, a stark contrast against the blue sky. When they neared a high country meadow, Mandy stopped the Jeep and pointed out a large herd of elk grazing. A stiff, cold breeze blew up from the valley to the crest of the hill.

Jenny sat up to see the large animals, until her dad noticed. Her expression changed, and she sat back against the seat.

Mandy longed to reach out and help her enjoy the vacation.

The animals had a darker neck and head area compared to the tan color of their hefty bodies. From the back, they were more visible with their lighter-colored rumps.

"Can we get any closer to them?" Rick strained against the seat belt with camera in hand.

"I'll drive over to that pull-off and you can get some better shots. The elk are docile this time of year, but you have to remember, an animal can be very unpredictable, especially a pregnant one and you never want to put yourself in a position where the elk feels threatened or their young are in danger. Those mommas will come after you if they feel they have to protect the herd."

Mandy drove up the hill that overlooked the meadow. Other than grasses, the only thing that remained were the gray stumps of trees cut in years past, or fell from wind and age.

Rick and Connie got out. Small yellow flowers growing close to the ground made Connie stop to take a picture, along with small white tufts of flowers. Lichen-covered rocks littered the area.

"Come on Jenny. Come see the elk."

She gave a dramatic roll of her eyes.

"Don't go any farther than that clump of scrub oak

over there, and watch your step." Mandy leaned against the front end of the Jeep.

Jenny got out and sat on a nearby rock. She plucked at the sparse tall grass blades and tossed them into the wind.

Mandy sent up a little prayer. "You know, when I was your age, I hated to go places with my parents."

"Yeah?"

"Yeah. It was so boring, and I didn't want to leave my friends. I bet you feel a bit like that."

"I do. I didn't want to come, but Dad said we needed some family time." Sarcasm dripped off the words. "We have that at home. I don't know why we have to do it out here. I'm homeschooled, so we're always together, well, except for Dad. He's always working. Even here, he's been working."

"You might be surprised how much fun you can have around this place. If you want, I could teach you something about horses while you're here."

"Really?" Jenny sat up. "I like horses. I've always wanted to learn how to ride." Then she slumped again. "But Dad said we need to see the sights. Do things together."

"How about we talk to them and work out some time with the horses. You're here for twelve days."

"Um...sure. I don't think Dad will let me, but you can try."

Mandy prayed that it could work out for everyone's benefit.

"Wow." Rick wore a huge smile as they returned to the Jeep. "We got some great shots. You can tell some of them are pregnant. When do they give birth?"

"Late June, sometimes July. The babies get spots just like a deer's fawn. If you watch them long enough, they play like any kids. Everything they do is for learning purposes. Every now and then, they'll come wandering through the main yard at the ranch. Barney doesn't even get up any more when they come through. He's so used to them. And they don't like to move for the Jeeps, so sometimes you just have to wait them out."

Mandy drove the family to her favorite spot for a picnic lunch. Craggy mountains perched high above the meadow in the distance. She pulled up next to a creek with green grasses waving. The steep peaks surrounding them protected the area from wind. The warmth of the sun allowed them to remove light jackets.

She pulled out the basket, blanket, and cooler that the kitchen staff had prepared.

A high waterfall came off the gray mountain to feed the creek below, near where Mandy settled the blanket and basket. Thick vegetation lined the water edges.

"This is the most amazing spot I've ever seen in my life." Connie whispered.

"Yes, I agree. We feel blessed to have areas like this so close by. This is our absolute favorite spot to picnic." Mandy laid out the sandwiches, chips, and chocolate chip oatmeal cookies.

Birds chirped and butterflies danced.

"What kind of bird is that?" Connie pointed down to the water.

"Oh, that's a Dipper, or Water Ouzel." The small black bird dove underwater only to pop back out several feet away.

"Jenny, can you see that bird? Isn't that funny? Look at him just dive under the water."

The girl uttered something unintelligible.

"I know you haven't signed up for the horses, but I wondered, we don't have a full booking this week, so if you want, I could work with Jenny in your free time and teach her how to ride," Mandy offered.

"Oh, I don't know..." Connie's eyes widened then looked to her husband.

"I'm not sure that's a good idea. Jenny's never ridden." Rick shook his head.

"Dad..." Jenny whined.

"We have very good horses. They're very used to rookies. I'm a great teacher and our wranglers are the best."

"Well, I guess you could try it."

"Really?" Jenny was thrilled. "I'll be careful Dad. I will. Mandy will help me."

They finished their lunch, cleaned up, checked the area for any trash, and loaded back into the Jeep. The drive back to the ranch held sights that were more incredible.

Mandy checked the rearview mirror and noted the faint smile on Jenny's face.

5

The Carter family had a pink tinge to their faces despite sun block. Exhausted from the excursion, Rick and Connie decided to go rest.

Jenny marched towards the pond and plopped down on a bench.

Mandy headed over to the office. "Hey, Sue. How's it going?"

"Oh, great. I'm just going through the mail. How was the ride?"

"It's beautiful out today. I took them up to Sugar Creek, and then picnicked up at the waterfall viewpoint."

"Oh, I love it there. I need to go up one of these days. I haven't been since last August. Now here it is half way through May. I'm having withdrawals."

"I know what you mean. I—"

"Mandy, what in the world....?" Sue handed her a piece of paper that had been crammed into the mail pile.

Stay away from the mine
Or there will be more fires and trouble.
You won't be going on with your plan.
Just back off and no one gets hurt.

"What is going on? Call Jon and tell him to get in here."

Sue radioed Jon.

He came rushing into the office minutes later.

"Jon, look at this."

Jon read it. "Call the sheriff, Sue. We have a definite problem here."

Sue placed the call and handed the phone to Jon. Jon asked the dispatcher to send the sheriff to the ranch to discuss the letter and the fire.

"We'll have to tell everyone to watch for anything suspicious or out of order. Sue, call the staff. Tell them there will be a meeting at 6:30 PM in the conference room."

"You got it."

Worry lines creased Jon's face as they walked to their home. Jon and Mandy had fallen into the habit of discussing everything on their porch, within view of the mountains during the warm months.

Mandy went inside for some cups and a carafe of coffee.

Within twenty minutes, the sheriff pulled in.

"Hey, Jon, Mandy. What's going on?" The officer extended his hand in greeting. Jon took his proffered hand. Mandy handed him a cup of coffee.

"Well, you heard about the fire this past week. Now we received this letter in the mail this morning." Jon handed him the paper and pointed to the chairs, inviting Ed to sit. "We also had a brake line possibly tampered with on one of the Jeeps."

"Hmmm…getting a little too intriguing isn't it. Anyone else touch the letter?" Ed dropped it into a clear plastic bag he had removed from his pocket.

"Just us, and Sue."

"Ed, I'm getting really concerned." Mandy leaned against the porch rail. "It's one thing to start a fire and run, but now to start threatening us to stop our plans...I just don't understand who would care so much. What purpose would they have? Would someone really have cut a line? That could have been deadly."

"I don't know, Mandy. Are there any other problems with people, besides Shonee? I know he doesn't like any plans you guys do. 'Course, he's not happy with much of anything. We've talked to him, but he's got an alibi for the fire. It appears his hip is acting up again too, so I don't think he would have been able to hike up to the area. And he sure couldn't crawl under a Jeep without notice. When Pete and I showed up to question him he got angry. We confirmed that he had been at the courthouse early that morning."

"You know us, Ed," Mandy said. "We get along pretty well with most everyone. That's our business. We've even tried to reach out to Shonee over the years, but he won't have any of it. We just keep our distance now and hope he'll tolerate us."

"The trouble started when we applied for a building permit." Jon responded. "We submitted our application to open up the mine after we make it safe, so guests can have a real old west experience. I don't know why anyone would care one way or the other."

"I'd like to head up there and take a look around if you don't mind."

"Of course not. We need to get to the bottom of this. Jon and the boys checked some, but didn't see anything besides the footprints. Maybe you'll have better luck."

"Great. I know you must have a lot to do, so I'll head up and let you know if I find anything."

Jon shook hands with Ed. "You're welcome to

come back for dinner if you'd like."

"Oh thanks, but I think Betty would have my hide if I don't get home for dinner tonight."

"OK, well, let us know if you find anything. And give Betty our love."

∂∽⊛

As evening shaded the sky, everyone began to gather around the large, open area Jon and the hands had built for groups.

Rustic log benches lined the edge. Log sections large enough to sit on stood closer to the fire pit for roasting marshmallows.

A couple of the ranch hands had started to play guitars. Another stoked up the flames. The guests came to join in as they all watched the sun go down. It was a time to sing, laugh, and relax before they all crawled in for a good night's sleep after a day of fresh air and fun.

It helped to hear what they liked and disliked in order to plan the next day and the weeks to come. After all these years of operation, there were few complaints.

Phil played a rousing rendition of *"She'll be Comin' 'round the Mountain."*

Jon could see the tension in Mandy's shoulders. He leaned over and whispered to her. "Relax."

"Can we sneak away and go for a walk?" Mandy whispered back.

Jon took her hand and they headed off towards the pond. The moonlight led the way without the need for a flashlight.

"I can't seem to stop worrying. Why would anyone threaten us to stop this project? How could this affect anyone else? We just want to keep our business fresh and exciting. I just don't understand who could be doing these things."

"I know hon. I don't get it, either. All we can do is trust God. Maybe this will be the end of it. We're kind of stuck until we can meet with the county again, anyway. Let's just focus on our visitors for now."

"You're right. I'm trying." Mandy leaned into him. "I'm really concerned for Jenny, the young girl from the Carter family. She has that early teen attitude of trying not to enjoy herself."

"Ah…" Jon wrapped his arm around her. "You've found a new mission. You've always had such a heart for teenagers."

"I remember being that age and the struggle with all the emotions. Remember when our Cindy was thirteen? What a challenge to raise a daughter with hormones charging constantly. Jenny is such a sweet kid. I hate to see her feeling so miserable. The parents seem nice and try to dote on her, but she just won't have any of it."

They made their way to a bench on the far side of the pond. As they sat down, Jon held her in both arms. They could see the campfire and they watched the gaiety of the animated singing. Phil stomped his foot and slapped his knee to the rhythm of the music.

"Isn't it wonderful how people can enjoy just sitting around a campfire, singing, toasting marshmallows…"

Then Jenny jumped up and raced off to the cabin, arms flailing.

The music stopped, but then started up.

After a moment, Connie rose and followed her daughter, disappearing into the shadows.

"Oh, no. I wonder what's happened now. That poor family."

Jon pulled her closer. "Don't worry honey. They'll work it out. Cindy always got over it. Jenny will, too."

"I know. It broke my heart then and it still gets me. It's a tough age to get through. For everybody."

Mandy rested her head on his shoulder, and they just watched the stars. The moon reflected off the surface of the gently rippling pond. A coyote howled in the distance, sending a message to another of the elusive creatures, who replied with a haunting wail. Crickets chirped all around them with an occasional frog joining the chorus.

The smell of pine wafted on the breeze.

6

The next morning, Mandy spotted Jenny at the corral with Barney. She stepped up on the bottom rail and leaned her arms over the top rail.

"I wondered where my supposedly faithful dog had gone this morning. Looks like you have a friend."

Jenny kept her eyes on the horses chewing on their hay. "He came out a while ago and just keeps sittin' there next to me."

"He likes people. Especially girls."

Jenny grinned. "I like dogs. They never make you feel bad."

"Yeah, not like people, huh?"

"Especially parents."

Mandy turned and looked at Jenny. "Anything you need to talk about?"

"No, I'm just tired of being treated like a kid. I'm not a kid anymore. I'll be fourteen in three months."

"It's hard for parents to let go of their little girl, sometimes. Things will get better. You want to try a ride around the corral?"

Jenny's face lit up, and she nodded.

Just as they were about to climb into the corral, Jenny's mom called out to her to come back to the cabin.

"I was just going to ride, *Mom*." Her emphasis on the last word took away any endearment.

"I need you in here now, Jenny!"

Jenny stomped off muttering, "They never let me

do anything."

"We'll do it another time, Jenny." Mandy watched her go, remembering a similar scene in her own life so many years ago.

⮞⮜

"Hey, Mandy. How are you today?" Sue was cheerful.

"Oh, fine. How 'bout you?"

"Good. We had more reservations come in for the first week of June. Another is for mid-July. We're filling up fast."

"That's great to hear." Mandy settled in to do her paperwork.

Connie Carter burst through the door. "Jenny's run off! Rick went looking for her." Connie's frantic look broke Mandy's heart.

"What happened? Where did she go?" Mandy asked in a calm tone, despite her racing heart.

"She ran up the hill behind the cabin. She was mad when I told her to pick up her room. She just started yelling about not getting to do anything and ran."

"I'll radio a couple of the guys. We'll find her. Don't worry. She'll be all right."

⮞⮜

Jenny scrambled up the steep hill. The brown pine needles were slippery. She could hear her dad calling, but she couldn't see him. She wanted to escape. To be left alone. As she ran faster, her lungs struggled for enough air.

There might be wild animals, but she didn't care.

She was tired of being told what to do. She was tired of not being able to do what she wanted. She was tired of being away from her friends, and especially tired of being treated like a child.

The trees were thicker now, but she continued to run. She pushed at bushes that scratched her arms. Suddenly the ground vanished. She dropped into an opening hidden by the ground cover.

Falling.

Her skin scraped against cold rock and dirt. Her body bounced down into the darkness. Rocks and small roots poked through and grabbed at her hair as she slid into the underground tunnel. She came to a stop when her tennis shoes hit a hard surface with a thud. Small pebbles and dirt tumbled into her back.

The darkness overwhelmed her racing heart. Panic elevated. The rising dust made her cough and coated her sweaty skin. Her body ached. She brushed at her arms and legs as she looked up. Branches crossed over the opening, blocking most of the sunlight.

A whimper escaped.

She could see a faint light down the tunnel. There seemed to be something, but she couldn't focus on it. Where was she? What had happened?

Jenny shifted from one spot to another, hands pushing the matted mess of hair away from her face; the dread of what could come from the darkness scared her. What if wild animals lived in here?

She crawled forward and maneuvered in the cave...tunnel, whatever it was...to where she was able to stand upright, but her head bumped on the dirt ceiling.

Was that a light down there? She rubbed at her eyes, wondering if she was really seeing something.

She whimpered again. Were there big spiders? Beating hands against her body frantically, the hysteria rose. Her scratched arms stung.

How would anyone find her?

What if a mountain lion lived down here? Did they live in holes? In caves?

She tried to climb back up, but with every step, she slid back.

Tears formed and her voice came out just above a whisper, "Dad?" Then louder, "Dad? Help me, Dad. Where are you?" Panic began to rise as she heard her own voice hollering for help, echoing in the dark chamber.

Screaming, she tried to crawl up the steep slope, clawing at the dirt as it rained down.

಄಄

After calling the available staff together, Jon sent everyone out to comb the forest and call for Jenny.

Even Barney tagged along, sniffing the ground and checking shrubbery.

Rick and Connie swatted at bushes, their expressions grim and fearful.

Mandy walked nearby, searching her own little grid.

The mine was up to the left, but they'd have seen her if she headed that way. There wasn't anything to the right except Shonee's property.

Mandy continued to call out, her fear intensified. Once again, she commanded Barney to find Jenny.

"Lord, please let her be all right," she gasped out while she climbed. "Be with her, Father; keep your angels around her. Help us to find her. Lead us in the right direction. In Jesus's name."

Barney's ears were attentive, eyes wide and searching. Stopping from time to time, he would raise his head and sniff the air. He wasn't a blood hound, but he was smart and knew the area.

The adults dotted the hillsides and called for Jenny, and then paused to listen. Nothing. They kept going. Time slipped away. Every minute built more fear and anxiety.

About fifty feet in front of Mandy, Barney suddenly stopped, his ears raised, his head cocked. He took off at a hard run, and then started pawing at the ground and barking.

"Jon. Everyone. Barney's found something. Come over here."

"Help!" A faint voice echoed from the earth.

Everyone ran towards Mandy.

Barney dug and continued to bark, his claws ripped the smaller branches right out of the ground.

"Jenny, are you down there?" Mandy hollered. Her heart pounded as she prayed for an answer from the girl.

"I'm down here! Get me out!"

"I've found her," Mandy called to the others. "Jenny, can you climb back up?"

"I don't think so. It's too steep. Please help me, Mandy." Jenny's voice trembled.

Jon pulled at the vegetation that partially covered the opening. "I've never seen this opening before. It has to be a ventilation shaft for the mine." He pulled away the grasses and stomped down the brush.

"Jenny. Sweetheart. Are you all right?" Her dad called down as he dropped to his knees to help clear the opening. "We're all here. We'll get you out. Just hang on."

"Oh, Daddy, get me out of here. Please?" Her whimpering was heart wrenching.

"Let me get down there." Nate offered. "These shafts usually run at an angle, so I should be able to help her get back out."

"How?" Mandy asked, a myriad of fearful possibilities running through her mind.

"I'll show you. Step back, Jenny." He called to the girl. Then, he went in. His long legs stretched from side to side as he climbed down.

The waiting searchers could hear the murmur of voices and then a few minutes later, Jenny's head popped out of the hole.

Hands reached for her and Barney's lapping tongue made contact with her cheek.

Connie grabbed her daughter into a tight embrace and cried. She pushed her back a bit to look her over. "Are you hurt? Are you OK?"

Jenny nodded, and then her face reddened when she saw everyone.

Barney rose on his hind legs and the girl petted him, breaking the tension.

"How did you find me?"

"You made a friend with Barney," Mandy said, putting an arm around Jenny. "He found you. I just followed him."

Jenny knelt down and put her arms around Barney's neck. "Thanks, Barney."

The dog leaned against the girl, wallowing in her attention.

"Jenny, you can't just run off like that. You scared us to death." Rick said, his tone stern, but his expression said something else...relief. He took her into a secure hug when she stood.

"I know, Dad. I'm sorry. I just got so mad…" she wrapped her arms around her dad tighter. "I was so afraid you'd never find me." She sobbed, unable to say more.

"I would never give up looking for you." A tear ran down the man's cheek.

Connie put her arms around them both. "Let's head back. We need to wash up some of those cuts."

As everyone walked down the hillside and returned to work, Jon grabbed Mandy's hand. "Crisis averted," he whispered fervently. "Thank God."

Yes, Lord…thank You. Mandy's relief made her feel able to breathe again.

7

Mandy pulled off her dirt-covered shirt. "That was scary. I'm so glad she's all right. Why have we never found that hole before, Jon? We'll have to search more over there. We can't have people falling into these shafts ever again."

"I know. I'll take a couple of the guys up and see what we're dealing with. We'll have to really comb over our hills and seal off anything we find. I can't believe we've missed that one all these years."

"I'm really getting overloaded with all that's happening lately. All of this at the same time? It's weird. And we have someone running around threatening us."

"We have to leave that part up to the sheriff, and most importantly, to God. Why don't we sit down and pray for a bit. I think we need a lot of divine intervention these days."

Jon gave thanks for Jenny's rescue, praying for protection, resolution, and peace to overflow the ranch.

It was the only way to get through their days.

⭒

Rick and Connie and their daughter, Jenny, stood together at the pond.

Mandy walked down to check on her guests.

Jenny rushed over. Scratches covered her face and arms, but the attitude of bored teen was gone. The girl threw her arms around Mandy. "Thank you so much for finding me."

Mandy hugged back. "I think Barney had more to do with it than me. I'm so glad you're OK. You're scratched up pretty bad. Does it sting a lot?"

"Only when Mom sprayed stuff on it. I'll be all right."

"We really do thank you for helping us find her," Connie said.

Rick's expression was stern. "Didn't you know about that hole?" His agitation was obvious.

"No, unfortunately, we didn't. We thought we'd been over every inch of our property. When you're in the mountains, these kinds of holes can be anywhere. When the gold fever was high in the 1800's, people dug anywhere looking for gold. Mines always need ventilation to prevent the buildup of gases. We think that's what she fell into. Jon and some of our staff will go around the perimeter of our property, work their way in and do another thorough search. We have a lot of acres to go over. Meanwhile..." Mandy looked at Jenny. "Try to stay within the ranch compound, OK?"

Jenny's face turned pink, and she looked down. "I will. I'm really sorry I ran off like that."

∽∾

Jon sent Phil into town for supplies, and then grabbed flashlights, some hand tools and the property map to mark the spot of the ventilation hole.

Nate and Mark saddled the horses, and all three headed out to do a thorough search of the section.

"Let's head over to the fence line and start from there. We're going to be busy all summer with this mission." Jon led the way.

"Why can't these kids just stay where they're supposed to stay? There are rules." Mark was perturbed.

"Kids are kids, Mark. They don't always do what they're told. Besides, we run a business here and we need to make sure it's safe."

The fence line ran along Mr. Shonee's property.

Jon spotted the man behind his house. They did their best not to draw his attention.

A gruff voice hollered out to them, "What're you doin' there?"

Jon raised his hand in greeting and rode closer to the fence. "Hello, Mr. Shonee. Just checking the property over here."

"Well, don't be messin' with my side or you'll be sorry."

"Yes, sir." Jon waved and turned the horse back to the guys.

"That sure is one cranky old guy." Nate shook his head.

"I don't know why you're so nice to him. He doesn't deserve it." Mark leaned against the saddle horn.

"Well, Mark, none of us *deserves* to be treated nice, but God's love is the only way to get through to someone."

"Yeah, yeah, yeah. I know. We're all worthless. We all need Jesus. I've heard it all before."

Nate pulled on the reins of the horse, and headed up the hillside to check out some heavy underbrush. Finding nothing, he returned to Jon and Mark.

"We'll just cover this northwest flank of the property today. I've got it marked on our map where

Jenny fell in. We'll have to get a heavy gauge screen installed over that. When Phil gets back, we'll figure out how to get that done. That will be tomorrow's project."

"Maybe we ought to explore in there a little before we seal it off. I sure thought I saw a faint light off from where she went in." Nate said.

"What do ya wanna do that for? We've got enough work to do. It's just an old hole leftover from the mining days. Just seal it up and keep people out of there." Mark did his job, but never wanted to do more.

"We'll see if we have time. There's still a lot to do at the barn for repairs. And there could be a methane problem in there. You don't want to mess with that." Jon referred to the deadly gas often present in old mines.

"I ain't goin' in there," Mark mumbled.

"Yeah, I guess you're right. Maybe my eyes were playing tricks on me," Nate said, but he was troubled.

At dinner time they headed back to the corral, having found no evidence of other holes, mine shafts or other dangers.

8

Mandy spent the afternoon teaching Jenny how to ride around the corral.

Connie and Rick watched from the rail.

After the lesson, Mandy showed Jenny how to brush Cookie, the horse. Jenny took to the task eagerly, wanting to know everything about horses, asking questions of Mandy as she worked.

Mandy walked over to Connie and Rick and leaned against the wood fence. She enjoyed watching the young girl's delight.

Jon, Nate, and Mark rode in.

Jon dismounted at the hitching post next to the corral. "Hey Jenny, how's it going? You got the full lesson today I take it."

"I sure did. That was fun. I like horses."

Some guests were coming in from their adventures in the Jeeps. Others came up, carrying their catch of the day from the pond.

One of the Reynolds's family's young boys ran over to the group at the corral. His pockets were overloaded causing his shorts to hang a bit long on the waist. "Hey. Wanna see my rock collection?"

David...no, this was Danny. "Sure, Danny. Let's see what you've found." Mandy said.

Danny pulled rocks out. He had pink granite pieces, pyrite, quartz and lots of plain old gray stones. "Oh, wait. I got a real pretty one. Where'd I put that?" He patted the pockets of his cargo shorts. "Here it is. I put it in a special place." He unsnapped a small pocket. The rock was less than a quarter inch square, but had a brilliant, red glassy look with sharp edges.

Rick's eyes opened wide as he bent down for a closer look. "Wow. Do you know what you have there?"

"Yeah. It's a pretty red rock."

They all laughed.

"Can I hold it?" Rick asked.

"Yeah, but you have to give it back 'cuz I found it."

"I will. I promise." Rick took the small crystal out of Danny's grimy little hand. "This is Rhodochrosite. A nice piece of it, too."

"Rodo what?" Mandy asked.

"Rhodochrosite. I'm a geologist. Most collectors consider Rhodochrosite to be the most beautiful crystal in the world. It's a very fragile mineral, so it isn't surprising this piece isn't very large. Do you know where you found it, Danny?"

"I dunno. I been finding my rocks all over. I think I found this up on that hill over there," he said pointing behind the row of cabins. "Or maybe...I'm not sure. I just like it. Can I have it back now, mister?"

"Oh, sure. Here you go. Take good care of that one. It's very special."

Danny dropped it back into his small pocket. He snapped it carefully again, loaded up the other rocks that had been on display, and took off running for his brothers.

Rick watched him go. "What kind of mining did they do around here?"

"Gold, mostly," Jon said. "We actually have an old mine on the property. It's to the southwest of here. The shaft Jenny fell in could have been ventilation for that mine. They found some gold in it in the 1880's, but it played out about 1896. We have it blocked off until we can firm it up. There's no telling how far in and down it goes. We've never explored it. One of our plans is to build a small old Western town for the kids to play near the mine. We hope we can shore up the entrance and a little ways in so the kids can really experience the old West."

Danny's family came up, led by the boy, who was telling them about the rock and gesturing at Rick. After a short explanation, the topic returned to the building of the town.

"We're hoping to start building, soon," Jon said.

"Well, we hope to build," Mandy interjected. "We don't know if it'll happen."

Mr. Reynolds asked, "Why not? Sounds like a fun idea."

"We have an unhappy neighbor and we have had a lot of opposition from him."

Mr. Reynolds raised an eyebrow. "Well, I'm a lawyer. If there is anything I can do to help, I could look into it with you. I know with these boys of ours, the more there is to keep them busy, the better. I think they'd get a real kick out of playing cowboy in a real town."

Jon put his arm around Mandy's shoulder. "Well, that's good to know. I'll certainly let you know if we need more legal help. As it is, we missed an appointment with the county judge because of a fire that broke out the morning we were supposed to appear to defend against the grievances of our neighbor. They are supposed to call about a new appointment. But the judge is pretty booked."

"Hmmmm…let me make a call. I'll see if I can do anything."

Jon thanked him and gave him the judge's name.

The group went their separate ways; most of them headed to the cafeteria for supper.

Mandy took Jon's hand, and they headed for their house. "God is really amazing. He puts all these people together in one place for a reason. We have a geologist and a lawyer here the first week of the season."

"It's like that human tapestry Pastor Bob always talks about. People get woven together to help each other out, sometimes. That sure was a beautiful stone that Danny found. I think I'll keep my eyes to the ground more often. I wouldn't mind a couple of those to add to our shelf in the office."

"I wouldn't mind a nice piece of jewelry with that stone…" She hinted with a mischievous grin.

9

The next morning the phone rang.

"Great," Jon said, after listening to the caller. "We'll be there. Thanks for calling."

"Who was that?" Mandy asked.

"Judge Markum's secretary. Apparently, Mr. Reynolds called and got them to get us on the schedule. We have another meeting Friday morning at nine."

"Oh my gosh. That's great news. Maybe we can get this settled and still begin the project this summer. Wouldn't that be terrific?"

"Let's not get ahead of ourselves. We still have to convince the judge that the work won't affect Mr. Shonee. Then we need to figure out how to keep that man happy while the construction is going on, if it's allowed at all."

"You're right. I just want to get this idea off the ground. I better head over to the office and see how things are going today."

❧

Mandy went out the squeaky screen door. Barney met her at the steps as she came off the porch. He had his favorite ball in his mouth and was crouched in play mode, his back half wiggling.

"All right. Drop it."

The dog dropped the ball at her feet, wagged his

tail and took his ready-to-run stance. She tossed the ball, and he took off. As she turned to head towards the office, she noticed Jenny standing down by the pond throwing rocks into the water.

Barney came back with the ball and trotted along beside her.

"Drop it." She picked up the ball and pitched it close to Jenny.

Barney ran after it and plowed into Jenny's legs. She yelled as she started to topple. Barney skidded to a stop and rolled over, exposing his belly. Jenny regained her footing and knelt down to scratch his stomach.

"Sorry about that," Mandy said as she walked up. "I didn't think he'd actually run into you."

"That's OK. I didn't fall in. But at least it would've been something to do."

"Weren't you scheduled for another Jeep trip today?"

"Yeah, but Dad got a call on his cell phone from work. He has to take care of some things before we can do anything."

"That's too bad. Well, why don't you go ask your mom if you and I can go for a ride? I'll take you up the trails if you want."

Jenny popped up causing Barney to do the same. "I'd love to do that. I'll be right back." Barney followed her.

Mandy walked back to the main lot.

Connie sat on the front porch of their cabin with a book. Jenny was animated as she sought her mom's permission. Connie saw Mandy and yelled, "Thanks, Mandy. She can go." The woman settled back into her chair and opened her book again.

Jenny bounded down the path with Barney close by her heels.

Several horses stood already saddled and waiting for riders at the corral. Gina, the main wrangler, was checking the tack.

"Hey, Gina," Mandy called out. "Can we take Cookie and Maggie out?"

"Oh, sure. They're ready. I'll get a helmet for Jenny." Gina headed into the barn and returned with a riding helmet and two canteens with water. She handed Mandy a cowgirl hat.

Jenny took the helmet with a scowl on her face. "Why do I have to wear this again?" she whined. "I don't want to look like a dork. I rode fine in the corral the other day."

"You have to wear a helmet if you're going to ride a horse here at the ranch."

"You're not wearing one."

Mandy took off her hat and turned it over for Jenny to see inside. "I have a special insert in my hat for protection. If you want to ride, you have to wear the helmet. That's our rule."

"Fine." Jenny slammed the helmet on her head. She rode around the corral for a few minutes to make sure she was comfortable with the reins and in the saddle.

"OK, do you feel ready to tackle a trail?" Mandy asked.

"As long as you don't leave me."

"I won't. Barney and I will both be with you."

"He gets to come, too?"

"It's pretty hard to leave him. He puts in way more miles than the horses do, but he loves to run with us."

Mandy mounted Maggie.

Jenny's face lit up with delight.

"Now, just stay relaxed and the horse will do what you want." Mandy instructed. "Remember that you're the boss. You're in control. Don't let Cookie think she can have her way."

"OK," Jenny's voice held a bit of hesitation. "It's weird without the railings around me."

"Don't worry, sweetie. She's very used to rookie riders. She'll be good to you. Just relax, keep your back straight and go with the flow of her movements."

Barney ran on ahead of them as he anticipated their direction.

"Let's head up that way. I'd like to check on the area where we had a fire last week."

"You had a fire?"

"Yeah, a couple of days before you all got here. The guys managed to get it out before it spread too much, but it sure scared us. See all the reddish colored trees back here?" Mandy pointed out.

"That's those beetle-killed trees, right?"

"Right. You remembered."

"Sometimes I listen."

Mandy laughed and headed up the hillside.

Jenny followed.

Once they got over the hill, Mandy pulled up on the reins. They sat there for a moment and looked at the charred mess.

"Wow. That really could have been bad. It stinks, too," Jenny half whispered.

The ground was black with rocks protruding above the burn. Charcoal climbed up the trunks of the smaller trees.

"Yeah, we were real fortunate. God looked out for

us," Mandy said. She tugged the reins and headed down the other side of the hill. "Do you want to see the old mine site?"

"Yeah, that'd be fun."

They rode to the west of the burn. Up ahead was the entrance of the mine. Wood and fencing covered the opening. A sign on the barrier stated in large red letters, "Danger. Do not enter."

After they dismounted, Mandy tied the horses to a partially fallen tree. She handed a canteen to Jenny.

"This is the old gold mine." Mandy pointed.

"Did they really find gold in there?" Jenny made her way up to the fencing, gazing into the gloom.

"They did. Not a terrific amount, but the original owner of this property found enough to keep him going several years. Once it played out though, it just wasn't worth pursuing. We want to turn this into part of the ranch experience for everyone. That flat area over there is where we want to build a miniature version of an old west town. Kid size. Then we hope to shore up the mine going in about fifty feet or so, just enough so families can see what these old mines were like."

"That sounds fun. When are you going to do that?"

"Well, that's the tricky part. We might find out Friday when we can start. Come on over here a minute." Mandy led Jenny to the right of the opening. The area went over some rocks and then dropped down as it opened up towards the highway in the distance. "See that house way down there?"

"Yeah."

"That's our neighbor and he isn't real happy about the plans. So we need to work things out so he won't be disturbed by the process."

"Why should he care? He lives way down there. This wouldn't bother him any."

"It seems that way. It's important to try to be good neighbors."

"Why? It's your property. He shouldn't be able to complain about what you do."

"The Bible says to love your neighbor as yourself. Sometimes that's hard to do, but we have to keep trying."

"Oh. I don't know much about what the Bible says."

"Doesn't your family go to church?"

"We did when I was little. But now, Dad is always too busy and Mom doesn't want to go without him. We went a few times by ourselves, but just when we'd make friends we'd move again because of his job." Jenny's wistful tone wasn't lost on Mandy. "That's why they homeschool me."

"You're sure welcome to join us on Sunday morning if you'd like and if your folks don't mind. There are lots of kids your age to talk to. I'd be glad to tell you more about the Bible if you're interested."

Jenny watched Barney, who was digging at the base of a rock where a chipmunk scrambled into a hole. "I don't know. Maybe."

Mandy sensed Jenny's withdrawal. It was time to change the subject. "I'm sure sorry about your fall in the shaft. That must have been scary."

"Yeah, it was. I kept thinking about what you said about mountain lions. I didn't want to get eaten. Then I worried about bats getting in my hair, and spiders..." She shivered. "It was just icky in there."

"Ewww...that would scare me, too."

"I'm just glad Barney led me to you." At the sound of his name, the dog came over and licked Jenny's face. Then he plopped down, panting from his explorations.

"I prayed so hard for you. We all scrambled around on the hills trying to find you. We were all scared. The more I prayed, the more I believed that God was taking care of you. I just hoped you weren't hurt."

They listened to the wind blowing through the trees.

"Do you really think God is real?" Jenny asked, looking up at the sky.

"Oh, I know He is. I can feel Him right here," Mandy pressed her hand to her chest. "The more you learn about Jesus, the closer you get to Him. He's my very best friend."

"So what's the difference between God and Jesus?"

"God is the one in total charge of everything. We're all sinners and needed a Savior, so God sent Jesus, His own Son, so that we could be with Him in heaven. He had to die for our sins because we could never be good enough. God hates sin."

"I don't think I'm a sinner."

"Really? Do you always do what you're told? Ever had a bad thought about someone? I know I have."

"Oh. Well, yeah, but I'm a good person most of the time."

"The Bible says we can't get to heaven unless we believe Jesus died for us. He went through a lot because He loves us. God wants all of us to be in heaven with Him. Someone had to pay the price for us to be with God. To clean sin away. Jesus did that. His death paid for our sin."

"Humph...I guess I never heard that before." She glanced at Mandy. "I played with my toys in church when I was little. I don't remember much about Sunday school."

"Maybe you should come to church with us, then. You could learn a lot more."

"Yeah, maybe. Guess I'll have to see what Mom says."

"Come on. Let's ride some more. We can talk later. Just think about what I said. God does love you, Jenny. He stayed with you in that hole. You just need to take some time to get to know Him."

10

Jon and Mandy woke early on the day of the hearing. "Let's pray that all goes well," Jon said.

Mandy took his hand and asked for peace in her own silent prayers, too.

Remembering the fire, Jon cautioned the staff to keep watch for anything unusual.

Nate went out early on horseback to look out for any activity where it shouldn't be; his main focus around the mine.

Jon and Mandy left early and had breakfast at the Sugar Creek Café, named for the old ghost town up in the hills. The restaurant's walls were covered with black and white photos of the town in its early days in addition to miner hats and tools. From the window, one could view the rust colored tailings of various mines that ran down the hills.

Toni, the waitress, set steaming plates of bacon and eggs on the table.

"Thanks Toni. I'm so nervous, I doubt I can eat."

"Now, Mandy...ya know ya need to eat! Cain't face the battle on an empty stomach."

"Mandy, you know you'll be sorry later when the stress hits hard and you don't have anything in you." Jon said. "Eat what you can."

"I made sure the eggs are how you like 'em. Now chow down."

"OK, OK, you two.."

Jon prayed over their meal and dug in. When he'd

finished all but his coffee, he pulled the briefcase up on the table and began rifling through the papers.

Mandy grinned. "How many times are you going to check that stuff?"

"I just want to make sure I haven't forgotten any of the pertinent papers. It looks like I have all the plans, drawings and legal documents. I guess I'm set."

"We can only do what we can." Mandy's gaze drifted to the window. "There goes Mr. Shonee. Guess he isn't about to miss this, either."

The man used his cane to hobble up to the steps of the courthouse.

"Well, let's finish up and get over there. I don't want to take the chance of him talking to the judge without us there, again."

Toni had spotted Mr. Shonee, too, and brought them the check. "We'll be praying for you over there."

"Thanks," they said in unison as they gathered up their belongings.

❧❦

Inside the judge's waiting area, Mr. Shonee sat with his hands crossed on top of his cane.

Jon greeted him and extended his hand.

Mr. Shonee grunted a response, but didn't take the proffered hand.

"Hello, Mr. Shonee." Mandy acknowledged him, too.

"I'll let Judge Markum know you're all here." The woman stepped into the office to her right, and closed the door.

The judge welcomed them into his office. Judge Markum lowered himself into a chair letting out a heavy sigh. "OK, now that we are all here this time, let's try and settle these disagreements. Mr. Phillips, I got a call from an attorney by the name of Reynolds stating your case for a new meeting due to a fire you had. I trust everything worked out all right in that regard."

"Yes, sir. Thank you for asking. We spotted the fire early enough and were able to get it out before it got out of control. That's what caused us to be late."

Mr. Shonee harrumphed.

"We do apologize for that, sir." Jon's voice was non-committal. "We know how busy you are, and we appreciate that you allowed us to come in today to try to resolve this. We hope to settle it without the additional assistance from our lawyer." Jon gazed at Mr. Shonee.

"There's nothin' to settle other than these people not being allowed to mess up the land and my peace and quiet."

Jon reached for the briefcase. "We have plans to build this project with very little disturbance to anyone in the area. I have maps and diagrams, as well as the blueprints for the project that detail how and where it will be done, including the property lines of Mr. Shonee's adjacent land." Jon pulled out the documents. He handed them to the judge and Mr. Shonee, who pushed them away.

The judge laid out the prints, and looked over the designs. He stood and leaned over the table to see the plan better, making "mm'hum" sounds as he perused the material. He then sat back down and paged through the other paperwork Jon had given him.

Jon took Mandy's hand under the table as they waited.

Mr. Shonee shifted in his chair.

The judge removed his glasses. "You have put great effort into this plan." He looked to Mr. Shonee. "What exactly are your objections to this project?"

Mr. Shonee straightened and began a litany of issues. "For one thing, this area that they want to build on is right above my house. I don't want my days filled with hammering, trucks, saws and other obnoxious tools disturbing my peace. I sit outside a lot, and I'll have to see all that going on for who knows how long. They want to mess around by the old Jackson mine. That's history for this area. It needs to be left alone. Ya can't go disturbin' history. Noisy machines are going day and night. It's bad enough all them dang kids run around there making all that noise. They had to dig that one girl out of the hole she fell into..."

Jon's eyebrows rose up. "How did you know about that?"

The judge's concern now joined in. "What is this about?"

"Yeah, see, it ain't safe on that property, and here they want to make more stuff to get kids in trouble with."

Mandy scooted forward in her chair. "Judge, everything is fine. One of our guests is a young teen and after a disagreement with her parents, ran off. She fell into an old ventilation hole that was unknown to us. We found her, and she's OK. We sealed the hole immediately. We now have our staff going over the property with the intent to find any other areas of concern that we might need to fix."

"Yeah, they've been messin' around near my property line and I don't like it. It's just plain dangerous and they shouldn't be allowed to do anything more."

Jon straightened. "We apologized to you that day. We are doing our best not to disturb you. We could just put up a huge fence and you wouldn't have to see anything anymore."

Mandy grasped his knee to calm him down.

"You better not dare to do that! I'm not going to have a big old fence ruining my view. I'll see you in cour—"

"Now, now," Judge Markum interrupted. "Let's keep this on subject. All of your plans look sound. As long as you correct any other problem areas, I don't see why this should disturb you, Mr. Shonee. The lay of the land looks like there will be little, if any effect on your peace and quiet. Several hundred yards and the elevation climb alone will diminish any noise issues. Efforts can be made by the crews to limit the noise and they won't work after sunset, so your evenings will be quiet.

"The actual site for the old style town is well to the backside of the mine and the hill would buffer the noise. Even when the guests enjoy the finished project, you most likely won't hear a thing. As far as the history, it is on their property. Ownership allows them to do what they want. I see no other reasonable objection that could stand in the way of this project. I hereby rule that the Phillips's, with High Country Safaris, have clearance for their plan, effective immediately. This matter is settled."

Mandy and Jon hugged, and stood up to shake the judge's hand.

Mr. Shonee sputtered as he tried to get more objections out.

Judge Markum held up his hand towards the older

man. "No, Mr. Shonee. This is settled. You will just have to deal with the construction for a little while."

Jon attempted to soothe the old man. "We'll make every effort to keep the noise level as minimal as possible."

The man struggled to get out of his chair. His face reddened. Muttering, he made his way out the door.

The judge watched him go. "Do your best by him. He won't be happy no matter what you do, so keep that in mind. Good luck. I think it will be a great addition to business in this town."

Jon thanked the man again and they left the office.

Mandy thanked the secretary as they passed by her desk and out into the hall. "We got it. We get to go ahead with our plan. Oh Jon, I'm so thrilled. I just didn't think it would happen. We need to thank Mr. Reynolds for his help in getting this appointment." She was so giddy with excitement, she almost jumped up and down. "Let's get back and let the staff know. Everyone is going to be so happy."

"We have a lot of work ahead of us, but we'll have so much fun. Let's go."

Mr. Shonee was cautiously making his way down the marble steps.

Jon tried one more time to appease their neighbor. "I promise there will be little effect on you, Mr. Shonee." Jon tried to take the man's arm and help him down the steps. "We'll do all we can to make it an easy experience for you. We don't want to be bad neighbors."

The man pulled his arm away. "Yer already bad neighbors. Leave me alone. You're gonna regret disturbin' me." He hobbled down the steps of the old courthouse to his car.

"I'm worried about him," Jon said.

"Do you think he'll do something to stop our project?"

"No...I just think he doesn't look well. He's so angry. That isn't healthy." Jon cared for people, even those who aggravated him, and his deepened concern for Mr. Shonee showed. "We'll just have to proceed carefully and do right by him."

Mandy hugged Jon. "I love your heart."

11

Mandy didn't mind getting up early on Sunday mornings. Seeing her church family and getting ready for new guests just made the day right. She went out the door and over to the office.

Sue attended church on Saturday nights, so she was always able to come in for the morning.

"Anything going on that I need to know about?" Mandy asked as she walked into the office.

"No, I don't think so. There're four more families coming today, but we'll get them registered and settled if they get here before you come back. All ready for church?"

"Yeah, but we've got an hour before we have to leave. I'm hoping that the Carters are awake. I invited Jenny to join us for church, but she's a bit hesitant. I'll go see if anyone is up and about at their cabin."

"OK, see you later."

The warm, Colorado sun was just coming up over the hilltops. The fresh smell of the air inspired a smile. A stellar jay squawked up above as it glided over to another Ponderosa pine. Deer grazed down by the pond.

Rick stepped out of the cabin, a cell phone to his ear.

She waved.

Rick waved her over, and then slid the phone back into the case on his hip. "Hi, Mandy."

"Good morning. How are you today?"

"Uh...good. Just wish the office would quit calling. I'd like to enjoy this vacation without interruption. It seems they can't keep our latest project going without my advice."

"Well, it's good to be needed."

"I suppose."

"Is Jenny up? We're heading to church this morning. You're all welcome to join us if you'd like. I had mentioned it to Jenny the other day."

"Church? Uh...well, let me go check." Rick went into the cabin.

Jenny came out followed by her mom.

"Hi, Mandy."

"Hi, Jenny, Connie. We're heading to church in about an hour, are you interested in joining us?"

"Oh, I don't think so." Connie looked at Jenny's attire. "Jenny doesn't really have any church clothes."

"Oh, jeans are fine at our church. We're more laid back here in the mountains. We get a lot of campers who join us Sunday mornings."

"Can I go Mom? We could all go." Jenny's gaze was hopeful.

"Well...you can go, I suppose. I don't think your dad would be interested. How long will you be?" She looked to Mandy.

"Only a few hours, counting drive time. You can join us."

"Oh, no, thanks, but Jenny can go."

"Let me grab my purse. I'll be right out." Jenny ran into the cabin.

"I think she'll enjoy it. We have a lot of teens in our church. She'll get to meet some kids her age."

"Oh, that would be good. Maybe she'll get in a better mood."

"You've got one more week here, so maybe we should help her get to know some of the teens who help us out around here."

"That'd be great."

"Bye, mom. See you later." Jenny called as she went down the path. She stopped to pet Barney, who rolled over on his back to expose his stomach.

"He's so spoiled," Jon said, sitting on the porch, sipping coffee and reading the newspaper.

"I like your dog. He's great."

"Jenny is going to join us at church this morning!" Mandy told her husband.

Jon's face brightened. "Oh, good. You'll like it, Jenny. There's a lot of kids your age there."

"Yeah, that's what Mandy told me." Jenny sat on the front step with Barney leaning against her leg as if attached to her.

"Let's get going, and maybe we'll have time to introduce you to a few kids." Mandy said.

Mandy took Jenny over to a group of teens by the front door. She knew all of them. Three of them were volunteer workers at the ranch.

"Hey, everybody." Mandy greeted them. "This is Jenny. She is one of our guests this week. Can you take her to Sunday school with you?"

"Hi, Jenny," several said in unison.

"Hi. I'm Dean. I think I saw you at the ranch last week."

"Yeah, we're on our second week here. But we leave next Saturday." Jenny shook his hand.

"You can hang with us this morning. We have a fun class."

"OK. Sure."

"You'll enjoy it." Mandy assured her. "The teen

class has more fun than should be allowed. We'll catch up with you afterward."

"Um...OK." Jenny went with the group. She turned back to look at Mandy, who just nodded her head and smiled.

12

The ranch became a flurry of activity Monday morning.

Jon and Nate left early to start getting supplies for the building up by the mine.

The road grader would arrive this morning to start leveling the area for the Old West town.

Barney leaned hard against Mandy's leg whenever she stopped to talk with guests and the ranch hands.

The tours were getting underway and various groups were climbing into Jeeps with their guides, piles of fishing paraphernalia, swimming gear, and hiking equipment.

As the vehicles drove away, Mandy sighed and headed for the office.

Barney went to his favorite spot under a couple of aspen trees.

Sue didn't come in until after noon, so Mandy had the office to herself. She clicked on the radio to her favorite local Christian station. The receiver for the radios mounted in all the vehicles voiced occasional static. Since cell phone reception was difficult, Jon had mounted a repeater on one of the taller hilltops in case of emergency. The repeater allowed the signal to be relayed across a wider area. Someone always monitored a receiver, whether in the office, the barn or the bunkhouse.

Mandy sat down at her computer after she started the coffee maker. Large windows looked out at the main parking area and the surrounding hills. She loved the view, but it sometimes hindered her work. Especially if deer or elk wandered through.

Later in the morning, Jon and Nate returned just as the road grader arrived. Jon, with the rolled-up plans in hand, led him up the hill to the site.

Mandy hoped they would be able to have lunch together today.

❧❦

Jenny picked up the last shirt off the floor in her room. Her mom insisted she clean it again. *Vacations shouldn't require cleaning.* She walked out into the open kitchen and slouched down into a chair. "OK, I'm done. Can I go for a walk, or do I have to do something else?"

Her mom sighed in exasperation. "No, you don't have to do anything else. You don't have to be so messy when we're at someone else's place. It doesn't hurt you to pick up after yourself. Go out, but don't go far and be careful."

Jenny grabbed her pink baseball cap and a water bottle and headed out the door. She stepped into the sunshine, relief filling her own sigh.

Barney spotted her. The dog's ears perked up and he came running to her.

She knelt down. "Hey, Barney. What are you doing today?" She scratched behind his ears. He plopped down in the dirt and rolled on his back allowing her to scratch his belly.

"You want to go for a walk with me, buddy?"

With a single bark, Barney took off.

"No, come this way. Let's go over here today."

He spun around and caught up to her.

She clipped the carabiner on her water bottle to the belt loop on her jeans and decided to walk along the deer trail that Mandy had pointed out. She didn't want to repeat her fall into a ventilation hole. Maybe she'd see that young deer that had been around camp.

The birds were chirping in the trees. Occasionally a small chipmunk scurried across the path. Barney would attempt to go after it, but she wouldn't let him chase the poor little thing. He came back when she yelled. Up on a branch, she saw a black squirrel with tufted ears holding a pine cone. It chewed pieces off and the debris fell to the ground.

She made her way around the base of a hill and noticed a fence line with a house beyond. She decided to turn a bit more uphill.

Barney traversed the hillside, sniffed at rocks and darted off to look behind a tree.

She stopped to take a drink of water. Barney made his way back, leaned against her hip and panted heavily.

"You thirsty, buddy?" She cupped her hand and poured some water into it.

He lapped it up, and then took off as another chipmunk scampered over a rock several feet away.

Jenny looked around, enjoying the quiet of the forest. The sun made it through the trees, but she was glad to sit in shade. She looked up at the deep blue sky. Only a couple of puffy, white clouds drifted by. "Are You really willing to be my friend?" She stared upward, waiting. Nothing came. "Come on, Barney." She stood and brushed the backside of her jeans. "Let's walk some more."

Barney ran off ahead.

A four-wheeler was parked near a small aspen grove. Jon, or one of the guys must be up here.

Barney was digging away at something, so she went on ahead. There were two machines parked, one with a small trailer behind it. Voices rose and fell in the air. One sounded angry.

Uneasy at the harsh tone, Jenny stepped behind a large ponderosa pine.

A man walked towards the trailer. He carried a pick ax with a heavy bucket in his other hand. He heaved the bucket up into the trailer and removed another large empty bucket.

Barney chose that moment to bark.

Jenny bent to silence him. She squatted behind the tree with an arm around Barney and stole a glance at the man.

He was running towards her. "What are you doing over there?" he shouted.

Barney barked frantically as he looked from man to girl.

Jenny started to run, but just like falling into the hole earlier, she slipped on the old pine needles. She scrambled up but a rock tripped her, and she slammed to the ground.

The man pounced on her as she attempted to get back on her feet. He grabbed her arms and pulled her up. "What are you doing here?" he demanded. He smelled like sulfur, sweat, and dirt.

"I...I was just out for a walk."

"What did you see? How long have you been out here?"

"N...nothing. I just got here. I...I didn't know who was over here. I don't even know who you are." Jenny shook with fear and tears blurred her vision.

As he yanked on her arm, Barney nipped at his heels and barked. The man kicked at the dog and made him yelp, and then dragged Jenny towards the vehicles. Barney lunged and bit him on the ankle. The guy hollered and slapped the dog away with one hand.

"Stop it. Let me go, you creep!" She tried to pull away and punched his arm with her other fist. "And don't kick Barney."

Another man stepped out of some brush into the small clearing.

"I know you. You work at the ranch. What are you doing? Tell him to let me go." Jenny demanded.

Her captor dragged her towards the hillside. Barney ran right behind them and continued to bark and snarl. "Grab that dog!" he growled to the other man.

Jenny screamed. Darkness showed through the gaping brush. Dread made her heart pound. She dug her heels in the dirt, pushing against his grip with her other hand.

The other man tried to grab Barney, who had begun a fierce growl, which turned to excited barking.

"Leave him alone!" Jenny screamed. "Barney, run. Go home, boy!"

Barney whined, looked at her, and then ran up the hillside digging in hard with his claws.

The ranch hand tried to run after the dog, but the slick pine needles and debris made it impossible. His feet slid back, and he landed on his hands and knees.

A scream escaped her once more.

"Forget the dog. Help me with her."

The ranch hand took hold of her other arm.

They dragged her towards the opening of the cave. She cried, trying to scream, but fear constricted her throat. Wood beams were set just beyond the entrance. She tried to grab one, but it was futile. The men gripped her too tight.

"What are we gonna do with her?" Ranch hand asked.

"I don't know, but we can't let her go. She'll tell someone we're here."

"I won't tell anyone." Jenny said through her tears. "I don't even know what you're doing. Just let me go."

The ranch hand let go of her arm and grabbed a lit lantern that sat just inside the entrance. He turned up the wick. Once beyond the entryway, the light illuminated a rough cut passageway that appeared to have been there a long time.

Up ahead more lanterns hung every fifteen feet or so. The passageway went deep into the hill. A dark abyss was beyond the lantern light. The man dragged her towards it.

Jenny struggled to break free of his hold. "You're hurting me. Let me go!"

"Knock it off or I'll really hurt you." He yanked her arm and followed the ranch hand.

They took another passageway, which branched off to the right. It narrowed.

The ranch hand grasped her arm, and handed the lantern to the tall man. He pulled her into the narrow slot, and Jenny had to use her free hand to protect her head as she stumbled along on the uneven floor. The tall man followed, hunched over, and blocked any escape.

The cave opened up. Tools and buckets were lying around and within the wall red crystals glimmered in the lantern light. The rock in the buckets was that rodo stuff that Danny had been showing off.

"Put her over there and tie her up while I think." The tall man barked out the order as he paced and ran hands through his unruly, dirty hair.

"Sit," the ranch hand said. He leaned her forward and tied her hands behind her back, then tied her feet at the ankles. "Just be quiet and do as you're told," he whispered.

Jenny fought back more tears.

"Come on," the tall guy roared. "Come outside with me. We've gotta get things out of sight in case anyone followed her." He limped out of the cavern.

"Don't leave me in here. Where are you going?"

The men ignored her and headed back down the passageway.

Only one lantern remained. The damp cold sank deep into her bones. She struggled against the ropes, but they didn't give. "Let me go!" Her scream echoed down the tunnel. Thoughts of bats, wild animals and these men sent shivers of terror down her spine. Through the tears, she sobbed words out loud. "God, are You here? I really need You right now."

13

Jon and Mandy sat on the porch of their home enjoying their sandwiches and discussing the town site plan.

"The excavator should be done this afternoon. The contractor is sending a couple of cement workers tomorrow morning to start the foundations. They'll have a lot of prep work to do, but things will start happening now."

"This is so great, Jon. Our dream is becoming reality. How long do you think it will take?"

"It'll be a month or two, I imagine. Once the foundations are set, the carpenter crew will come in. Our design is for six structures, and being miniature, it could go fast. We should be able to start some fun events for the kids by July. We can dress up the front of the mine and still keep people out of it, but make it look Old West. Once the fall season comes, it will be a better time to work on shoring up that entrance better. I've put in a request to the Colorado School of Mines offering their senior design students an opportunity to do some studies there if they can shore it up."

"That's a great idea. They'll probably jump on that offer."

"I hope so. We'll have to—" Loud barking interrupted Jon as Barney ran full speed into the yard.

"Barney, quit barking." Mandy went out to him.

The dog barked, spun in circles, and jumped up, twisting.

Jon got Barney's water dish from the porch and put it in front of him.

The dog lapped at the water, and then started barking again. He ran in the direction that he came from, looking back at them. Then he circled behind them, as if herding, and ran towards the hill again.

"What is wrong with him?" Mandy asked.

"I don't know. Maybe he just spotted a cougar and it scared him. His way of telling us about it? I don't know. I've never seen him act like that before."

"Weird."

⋰⋱

The sounds within the cave were muffled but Jenny thought she heard the machines drive away. What was going on? Why were they doing this to her? Why couldn't they just let her go? She wished she could remember the one man's name.

Looking around, she noticed spots where they had dug into the walls. Some of the niches reflected the light, intermixed with deep red crystals. They were beautiful. Despite the pretty stones, the cave smelled dusty, and it was cold. Her stomach growled.

A familiar bark echoed.

"Barney?" She called out.

The next bark was closer.

"Barney, here, boy. I'm here. Come here, boy!"

Barney appeared in the opening. Alone. He went to her and started to lick her face. She could only turn her head from side to side in an attempt to avoid the tongue on her lips and nostrils. "OK, Barney. Good boy. Man, am I glad to see you."

He sat and looked at her as if wondering why they

didn't go back out to play.

"I don't know what to do, Barney." She leaned to the side to show her tied hands as if he'd understand what that meant. "I can't get these ropes off and those guys left, and I don't know why I'm here, or how I'm going to get out of here. No one even knows where I am. And I'm getting hungry."

Barney's head tipped from side to side.

Grief filled her throat as the words left her. Tears fell again.

Barney whined and snuggled closer.

"At least my buddy came back. You're my friend aren't you, Barney?" He rested his chin on her knee. The thought came back to her about Jesus being a friend. With a gulp she whispered, "Is that what they meant?

"Jesus? Are You maybe...here...right now?" Goose bumps rose on her arms. She dropped her chin and closed her eyes.

Barney pressed his back against her leg.

"Jesus, I don't know what's happened here, but I'm scared. Jon and Mandy said I could talk to You, that You wanted to be my friend. I know I've done a lot of things wrong and I'm sure sorry I stumbled on this today. I'm in another hole and I can't see any way out. I'm glad Barney's here, but I think I need Your help more than his. Can You please protect me and get me out of here? Please?" She raised her head and looked to the ceiling.

Silence.

More tears fell.

⤞⤝

"Oh, here come the Carters." Mandy said, as she

picked up their lunch dishes.

Jon laid the papers he was looking over on the table and stepped off the porch to greet their guests. "Hi, Connie. Hi, Rick."

"Hey Jon, Mandy." Rick walked up. "Have you seen Jenny? She went out for a walk and hasn't come back yet."

"We haven't seen her all morning." Mandy replied. "What time did she go out?"

"Several hours ago. I don't know why she isn't here." Connie's concern was etched in her expression.

"I'll get on the radio and see if anyone has seen her." Jon headed for the office.

"Have you looked around yet?" Mandy asked.

"No. We thought she must have gone for lunch at the cafeteria, but she wasn't there. I've called for her, but nothing."

"Do you know which way she went?'

"No, I don't. Oh, Mandy. She got a bit upset this morning when I had her clean her room again. She went out on her own, but she wasn't mad when she left. I don't know where she could have gone."

"Don't panic, Connie. You know, Barney ran back here all excited a little while ago. I bet he knows where she is."

Rick looked around the property. "Where did he go, then?"

"Well, he ran off in that direction. Tell you what. I'll go get my horse and ride out that way. She's probably enjoying the woods. Why don't you check around here and just wait in case she comes back. Don't worry, everything will be fine." Mandy said the words with more confidence than she felt. A few minutes later she mounted her horse and headed off to the west of the ranch. She now regretted that they ignored the agitated dog.

She called out for either one of them. There was no answer and no sign. "Lord, where are they?" she prayed out loud. "Father, whatever is going on—once again, Lord—please protect Jenny. Lead me to her. And I also ask, Lord, that Barney is all right, as well. In Jesus name…"

She followed the deer trail, winding around the edge of the hillsides. She continued to call out Jenny's name. The forest seemed even quieter now. It felt eerie. She kept on riding, looking, calling, until she heard a very cranky voice.

"What's all the darn noise over there about, now?" Mr. Shonee hobbled towards the fence line.

Mandy pulled back on the reins and groaned. She turned the horse towards the man. "Hello, Mr. Shonee. I'm sorry to disturb you. We're just looking for a young guest. She hasn't returned from her walk this morning and we are getting a little worried. You haven't seen her, have you?"

"You lost someone again? I haven't seen anybody, but I'm darn tired of listening to all that racket over there. You people are just trouble. Noise, losing people, I don't know how you stay in business. They ought to just shut you down. Quit making so much noise and leave me alone." The old man turned and stomped off as best he could with the cane.

"Mr. Shonee!" Mandy jumped down off her horse and marched over to the fence. "Why do you have to be so cantankerous all the time? I just asked for your help. You don't need to be so mean. We have tried to be good neighbors, but you make it so hard."

Mr. Shonee turned around, his craggy old face

reddening. "I've had enough of your lip lately. You'd be a good neighbor if you'd just move away." With that, he turned and headed for his house.

Mandy felt the heat rise up, her fists tightened at her side, and words were about to spill from her lips, when an overwhelming thought pushed to the forefront of her mind, *Be slow to anger. For man's anger does not bring about the righteous life that God desires.* The verse from James slammed into her thoughts. "Sorry Father. I should not get so angry with such a lost man." She took a deep breath and quietly got back on her horse. She reined the horse away from the fence and prayed for the man's heart to soften.

"Well, Maggie," she patted the horse's neck. "Let's head back. I doubt Jenny could have gone by here without Mr. Shonee seeing her. Let's head over to the old mine and see if she went up that way again."

14

Jenny jerked awake. "Huh, how long have I been asleep?"

Barney raised his head and looked at her.

"Oh my gosh. It wasn't a dream, was it Barney?" Fear gripped her heart as she looked around. There was another small passageway off to her right. There were mountain lions and who knows what else in these parts. Were there bears here, too? Bats? A shiver went through her body. The thought of spiders totally wigged her out, and she shook her head to get the suspected creatures out of her hair.

Jenny stretched her neck in every direction trying to loosen the tightness. Pondering her situation, she leaned over on her side and attempted to work her rear end through her arms to bring them to the front of her body. It took a lot of effort before she could finally work her body through, her long legs proving to be the biggest challenge. Her hands were now clasped in front of her, still tied, but now she could move better.

She pushed upright, unclipped the water bottle from the belt loop and got a drink. She offered one to Barney, and then began working the knot at her ankles.

A loud roar sounded. The machines were coming back.

She frantically pulled at the rope. She couldn't budge the knot.

Then the voices drew nearer.

The taller man came into view first. "Still here, eh?

And that stupid dog came back." Then he noticed her hands. "Tryin' to leave us?" He bent down and checked the knots as Barney growled at him.

She cringed. "Why are you doing this? Just let me go." Jenny had to turn her face away from the smell of his breath.

"I'm afraid we can't do that," he said with a sneer.

The ranch hand came through the passageway and walked to them. He held a brown paper bag out to Jenny. "Here," he said. "Something to eat."

Tears welled up. She reached out and took the bag with her tied hands. She removed a sandwich from its wrapper and eagerly began to eat.

The men moved away, talking in hushed whispers.

"What are you going to do if you aren't going to let me go?" Jenny asked when she'd finished the sandwich.

"Shut up! You'll find out later. Maybe we'll just put ya to work in here."

"Work? Doing what?" Fear and dread took over.

"Finding me some perty rocks." The tall man leered.

"Let's just let her go," the ranch hand whispered. "This was not part of the deal."

"Shut up, Mark."

She strained to hear more.

"We've gotten a lot of crystals already. Let's just get out of here. We're going to really have trouble now that we have her. There're gonna find us."

"Quit yer whining. I'm not giving up until I've got everything entitled to me out of here. Get to work. Get her over here and show her what to do. Don't untie her. She can work with the ropes on."

"How's she gonna do that?"

"I don't care. Just make her work."

Mark helped Jenny to her feet.

Barney kept a low growl and never took his eyes off the man.

Mark pulled her up and half dragged her to the area they had been excavating.

"The rope's cutting into my ankles," she said.

"Sorry," he whispered and slowed down.

"Sit her down over here. She can sort through the bucket. Ya better be dang careful too." The tall man glared at her. "Don't be bustin' the pieces up. They break easy, and if you want out of here, ya better do it right. Got it?"

She managed to sit, her feet to the side.

Barney sat down between the men and Jenny. She reached over with her bound hands and scratched his side.

Mark instructed her how to sort the best pieces and put them in a single layer in the tray beside her. The pinkish ones were to go to another tray. None of the stones were very large, but they were all beautiful, ranging from pink to red.

"What's so great about this stuff anyway, that you have to sneak around and kidnap me?"

Mark turned to her. "Rhodochrosite is worth a lot. It's as good as gold. Red gold."

"Never mind," bellowed the other man. "Just keep working. We're gonna have to finish up soon now that she found us. Then we got to decide what to do with her."

Jenny got back to sorting, terrified about what was going to happen next. Her hands were shaking, as she placed the crystals in the trays. Were they going to let her go when they were all done? She tried to pray, but it was hard when she was so afraid, and she wasn't sure how to do it right.

∂∘∽

The Carter family, Jon, Mandy and the sheriff were in the Phillips' living room.

Connie paced.

Rick's frustration had turned to anger. "I don't understand why she hasn't been found. What are you all doing? What if she's hurt in another blasted hole on this property?"

Connie gasped, and then sobbed into her hands.

Mandy put her arm around the woman's shoulders. "We've had every available staff member going over the property and no other ventilation holes have been found. The one she fell into has been sealed."

The sheriff spoke up, "Are you sure she wouldn't have run away?"

"No. She was fine when she left. She didn't like having to clean her room, but she wasn't that upset. She said she was just going for a walk."

"And you say Barney is missing, too?" the sheriff asked Jon.

"Yes. He showed up visibly agitated, and then took off again. We just didn't think that much about it at the time."

Rick's face turned a deep red. "Well, maybe you should have!"

"You're right. We should have, but in all fairness, Barney gets excited when he sees a chipmunk. He acts exactly the same way when he wants us to walk in the woods."

"We'll find her." The sheriff put on his hat and went out the door.

Rick stomped off to their cabin muttering about finding her himself.

Connie barely acknowledged the departing sheriff. Shoulders quivering as tears ran down her face, she followed her husband back to the cabin.

A car pulled up. Dean, from the church youth group, got out of the passenger seat as his dad hopped out of the driver's side.

"We heard in town that Jenny was missing. We came out to see if there was anything we could do to help."

"Oh, Carl, Dean. Thanks for coming out. You didn't see her in town by any chance, did you?" Mandy stepped off the porch to give them each a hug.

"We checked at the church and even the park. She's not there. More of the church families are heading out to help search. Do you know which direction she went?"

"Not really. We've got staff going up into the forest service land to search. The sheriff called the rangers. The sheriff has people out driving, too. I rode off to the west, but there's just no sign of her anywhere, or Barney, for that matter."

Another car pulled up that they didn't recognize. A young man got out with a notepad in hand. He stepped up to the group and introduced himself as a reporter from the local newspaper.

"We heard talk in town that one of your guests is missing. I'd like to ask you a few questions."

The sheriff, in the process of getting into his vehicle, stopped the reporter. "This isn't a good time for you to be here. Why don't you just head back into town?"

Rick had walked over. "Wait a minute. If this got in the paper, it could help. More people could look for her." Jon took the reporter aside and explained the situation to him.

Mandy prayed. *Keep her safe, Lord, protect her, and help us find her...*

15

Jenny shifted as much as the ropes allowed. "I have to go to the bathroom."

Mark came over to her. "I'll help you get up. You'll have to go down that passageway."

She grimaced as she looked in the direction he pointed. "But it's dark..."

He lifted her by the arm, and she struggled to gain her footing with her bound ankles. "I can't...go with my feet tied."

Mark looked to the other man.

"Fine. Untie her." The tall man stepped over to her, way too close for her comfort. "But if you think you can try to get away, you better think twice about it. I will come after you."

Mark led her towards a low passageway in the far wall. He handed her a flashlight. "You'll have to make your way down there. It goes nowhere, so you can't get away down there. Watch your head. Do your business, and come back out here."

Jenny shone the light down the low passageway. She would have to double over to fit. *I hope there aren't any spiders...* She found an area far enough so the men wouldn't see her. She looked around one more time and turned off the light to take care of things.

Barney stayed a few steps away.

Mark was waiting when she came out.

She felt a new wave of discouragement.

He tied her up again, a little looser this time, and

helped her sit down in her work area.

Jenny continued sorting the specimens, admiring the beautiful crystals. Most clung to other dark gray or black rocks. Even more had clear quartz mixed in. The pink ones were the prettiest and she held them a little longer, admiring the color. She wiped tears away on her sleeve.

A fragile red piece fell off a host rock. Jenny's heart pounded, but Mark and the tall man didn't notice. Her cramped position and the coolness of the cave added to her discomfort.

There had to be a way she could escape. *Are they even looking for me?* If only Barney would get help, but he was glued to her side. She didn't want him to leave, anyway. The warmth he radiated against her leg was a lifeline, holding her together. Tears filled her eyes again. She'd never been this scared. Never.

෴

Evening approached.

Volunteers had combed the hills in every direction, even members of the Alpine Rescue Team had been called in, but soon darkness would put a stop to their efforts.

Mr. Shonee was in his yard shaking his cane at the vehicles going past his house. He'd even called into the dispatch office of the sheriff's department to complain. He called over to the ranch to complain as well.

Mandy listened as Sue tried to explain there was a search going on for the missing girl, but his attitude got so belligerent that she hung up on him. Why did that man have to continually cause grief?

As twilight set, many members of the church

family began to gather in the parking lot of the ranch. Mandy knew the professional searchers would stay out in the wilderness, but they couldn't expect these families to stay out in the elements. She thanked them for their help and offered them dinner at the cafeteria.

Connie sat on the step of her cabin, head in her hands, sobbing uncontrollably.

Rick's own search came up with nothing. He stood, patting his wife's shoulder, his back hunched and his head down.

The volunteer searchers came out of the cafeteria in groups, standing around the corrals, the office, and the yard. A few people left to go home and take care of chores, but eventually they returned as the shadows lengthened.

The searchers joined hands, and Carl, Dean's dad, said a prayer. People stood, their silent vigil the only support they could offer.

෨෧

The two men wrapped up for the night.

Mark helped Jenny move back over to her original location. From a cooler they had brought in, he took out another wrapped sandwich and a few other items along with a bottle of water. He gathered up a couple of old scratchy wool blankets and set them next to her.

"What are you doing?" Jenny asked with wide eyes. "You're not leaving me in here tonight are you?"

"I don't have any choice," Mark whispered. He added another rope around her hands, attaching it to a heavy metal stake driven into the floor of the cave. Mark set a lantern nearby and turned the wick down low.

Panic increased. She did not want to be alone in this cave all night long.

Barney growled, as if he sensed Jenny's fear.

The taller man stomped towards her. "You better be here when we get back in the morning. We know how to find you and we know who your family is, so don't be stupid."

Terrified, Jenny could only cry.

Barney followed them out.

Her control fled. She wailed, frightened beyond belief. Finally, her body could take no more and she wound down. "You...you...you...can't leave me in here!" The wobble in her voice shocked her as it echoed back.

Barney trotted back in and lay near her outstretched legs, his warmth lessening the chill that permeated the room.

She raised her hands and began working at the knot with her teeth. The knot held tight. She reached down and attempted to pull at the rope around her ankles. She couldn't do it. The knots were just too tight.

Barney watched her every move.

"Barney, you gotta get help. You've got to go get Mandy."

The dog whined at the name of his master.

"Barney, go! Get Mandy!" She thrust her arms in the direction of the opening. The dog put his head on his front paws. His big brown eyes just looked up at her.

❧❦

Mandy stepped out of the shower. She hadn't slept much. Barney's absence disturbed her, as well. She prayed that he was with Jenny and providing some measure of comfort. She heard the screen door slam.

Jon marched up with the newspaper scrunched in his hand. "Look at this," he thrust the paper towards her. "Look what that reporter wrote."

"Young Teen Missing From Local Resort."

The article stretched into dramatics.

"Apparently, several safety issues have become a great concern for guests of High Country Safaris. Two serious incidents in less than a week have marred the ranch's ability to provide the fun adventure that they advertise. This type of adventure is not one any parent would want for their child. Where is Jenny Carter? Will she be found safe? The search continues. If you have any information about this teen, call local authorities."

Jenny's photo also appeared next to the article.

Mandy walked outside with Jon, startled to see many of the church members outside.

Dean came over to them. "We sent several people home, but the ones who wanted to stay slept in their cars."

"Would you like breakfast and some hot coffee? The cafeteria is open." Mandy was so touched she could barely speak.

"That'd be great."

After she got the kitchen crew started on feeding the crowd, she went back outside.

Mr. Shonee pulled up in his mint-condition antique luxury car.

"What on earth would he be doing here?" Mandy

asked as Jon came over to her.

"I want to talk to you two," the old man shouted, pointing his cane at them. "I saw the paper this morning. What's wrong with you people? You can't seem to keep track of anybody. I'm tired of all this traffic and noise. You got people crawling all over the place. Cars comin' and goin' are stirring up so much dust, my house is covered in it. You got them dad-blame machines running up the hills day and night. I keep gettin' bothered by cops questioning me all suspicious like. Even that fool reporter came knockin'. Then your dang office woman hangs up on me. I finally get my good-for-nothin' son out of the house and now I gotta deal with all this? I want all the racket and commotion stopped, and I want it stopped now."

"Mr. Shonee, we have to do all we can to find this girl. I should think you would want to help." Jon's words were terse.

"Blast. What am I gonna do about it? She's probably just another runaway. I want peace and quiet around here. I've lived in these parts for more than fifty years, I don't need all this."

"We're doing our best, Mr. Shonee," Mandy said. "Please, just be patient. You might want to think about saying a prayer for this young girl instead of being so angry about it. She's been missing all night."

"Prayer. Bah. Fat lot of good that would do me, or her. Just settle it down over here." The old man hobbled back to his car and his tires kicked up rocks and dirt as he left their driveway.

Jon watched him go with his hands in his pocket. "Sad old guy, isn't he?"

"Sad and infuriating. Let's go over to the office and see if any news has come in from the sheriff's office."

Sue was on the phone, trying to reassure the caller. She kept trying to say something, but was cut short with every attempt. She set the handset back down. "Hi guys. Umm...bad news. We've had three cancellations so far this morning. Folks are seeing the article and getting worried enough to cancel. And demand their deposits back."

Jon plopped down in a chair and cradled his forehead in his hand.

"I thought that article would help." Mandy began to pace. "Now look what's happening. We needed people to focus on finding Jenny, not think our resort is a danger to their family. What are we going to do? If we get too many cancellations, we won't even be able to keep the staff on. We can't let people go. They depend on us."

"The sheriff called to see if she had shown up during the night." Sue shuffled papers on her desk. "They've still had no sign of her. The rangers also called. No trace of her but they are still searching. Nate came in very early wondering where Mark has been. I guess he hasn't been around since two days ago."

Jon looked up. "Has he called in?"

"Nope. That's what's so strange. The guys know they have to call so we can get someone to fill in for them if they have a tour scheduled. Mark was supposed to lead a couple of guys on another fly fishing excursion this morning, so Ken had to take them up. He did say he'd be keeping an eye out for Jenny up by the lake."

"I think the three of us better just get to prayin' this morning," Jon said, his tone bleak. "Sue, come on over to the couch with us."

The three huddled and held hands, each one taking a turn to pray aloud that they would find Jenny safe.

16

Jenny woke up with the warmth of Barney next to her body. She was thankful for the heat and the company. The scratchy woolen blankets had barely covered her. She pushed upright and rubbed her sleep-filled eyes with the backs of her bound hands.

The lantern had dimmed.

She'd woken several times feeling like something crawled on her legs or arms. Another time a noise had made Barney jump and caused her to jolt awake. Tears fell every time she woke up. She groaned and sobbed at the memory of those scary nighttime hours and the realization of her plight.

She heard the noisy machines as the men returned to her prison. Relief came over her, along with dread. What was she going to do? She had to find a way to escape.

The noise stopped.

There were footsteps, and then they appeared at the opening.

"Ah...there's our girl," the taller man sneered. "Sleep well?"

"You've got to let me go. My parents are probably going crazy. This isn't doing you any good."

"Apparently your parents are going crazy. The whole area is crawling with cops, rangers and a whole lot of other people. We had to come in through my...the other property."

"This isn't fair." Tears fell again. "I want to go

home. I'm hungry and these ropes hurt. Please don't keep me in here any longer. I won't tell anybody that you're here."

"We'll keep you as long as we need to. Quit your whinin'. I don't want to hear it."

Mark had two sacks and a six pack of water bottles. He handed her the sacks and a bottle of water. There were snack bars, a couple of sandwiches, and bags of chips. The other held her favorite—glazed donuts. She pulled one out and began eating, sharing with Barney. "Can't you get me out of here?" she murmured to Mark.

He threw her a look of warning. "Shhh...," he whispered. "I'm trying to figure out something."

She leaned back against the cold rock wall.

Mark took up the lamp to fill it.

"It was really cold in here last night. These blankets stink. Can you get me something warmer?"

Mark pulled an old dark blue sweatshirt out of a plastic crate, shook dirt and dust out of it, and gave it to her. He untied her hands.

She rubbed her freed wrists, and then pulled the dirty shirt over her top. "I have to....go, too."

Mark untied her feet. "Come on. Back down the tunnel."

He had to help her up. Her legs were stiff and weak from being in the same position for so long. Her feet tingled as she tried to walk.

Barney stayed right at her side.

She stretched her legs, arms, and back in the tunnel. Relief accomplished, she made her way back to the main cavern.

The men were examining the vein of mineral.

She stepped quietly to the opening. If she could

just run as fast as she could...

Barney looked up at her.

She reached down, scratched behind his ear, and placed a finger to her lips. She looked at the men one more time, and took off at a hard run. Fire broke out in her lower limbs but she kept going. She had to get out of there.

Barney ran with her.

"Get her!" The tall man yelled.

Barney barked.

The uneven floor caused her to sail forward, feet scrambling for a hold.

The men caught up just as she was about to fall.

She screamed as the tall man grabbed her arm and pulled her to a stop.

Barney barked ferociously, but kept his distance.

"Dang it, girl. Don't be messin' around like this. You ain't goin' anywhere. Get that dog," the taller man yelled at Mark.

"Barney. Get out of here." She tried to wriggle from the tight grasp. "You've got to get out of here, Barney. Go get Mandy. Go!"

Mark made a move towards the dog.

Barney barked and growled at him. His teeth were bared, and he looked ready to rip flesh.

Mark continued slowly moving towards the dog. "Come on, Barney. Good dog, come here, buddy." The dog backed up and continued to growl, his teeth threatening the man. "Kane, he won't come to me."

Kane dragged Jenny away.

She screamed again, "Barney, run. Get Mandy." Crying overtook her.

The dog whined loudly, and then ran out the entrance of the cave.

Mark took off after him.

Kane pushed Jenny down to the floor and tied her up. The ropes cut into her skin. She cried out in pain.

"You ever try that again and you're gonna be so sorry." His face had turned red, veins in his neck stuck way out, and extended purple lines down to his shirt collar.

Mark returned without Barney. "The dog got away."

"Dang it, Mark. Can't you do anything right?"

"We gotta get out of here, Kane."

"Shut up, you idiot."

Jenny swiped at her runny nose with the sleeve of the sweatshirt feeling the grit stick above her lip.

"Seriously, Kane. It's time. We've gotten a lot of great gems out of here. We gotta let her go and get out of here. They're gonna find us, and then we'll have nothing."

"Dang it." Kane stomped over to the vein and took a serious look at what remained. He held the lantern up against the wall.

Jenny could see that dull greens, shiny silver areas, and white quartz-like rock remained. She saw the slightest amount of rosy pink.

Kane set the lantern down, rather roughly, startling Jenny with fear that it would break and burst into flame.

"If she wouldn't have messed it up for us, we could have dug in further to see if this vein picked up again. Dang it. I deserve this stuff. It's mine." He stomped over to the center of the cavern and looked around. "Get anything that might give us away and get it out to the ATV."

The men began going through the supplies.

"She already knows who I am, Kane. What am I going to do?"

"We'll just have to get out of the area. Grab this stuff and let's go!"

"You're not going to leave me in here, are you?" Panic rose in Jenny's chest.

"Shut up. You can be stuck in here forever, for all I care."

Jenny looked to Mark, silently pleading for help.

"Kane, we can't leave her here. She'll die. Then we're up for murder. I'm not going down for something like that."

"I. Don't. Care." He got in Mark's face, and then made his way out of the cave with a box.

Mark rushed over to Jenny and began to loosen her ropes. "Listen now," he whispered. "I'm going to loosen these up enough for you to get out of them. When we're gone, you'll be able to pull out of them and get out of here. Just wait until we're gone. He's real mad, and I don't trust what he might do to you." He frantically pulled at the tight knots until he had them much looser. Hearing footsteps in the passageway, he returned to sorting through things just as Kane reappeared.

Jenny pulled her feet up so they were harder to see. She could feel the rope almost falling off. Her hands were hidden in her lap. She fought to hold back the tears.

Both men left the cavern with more crates and equipment.

Jenny examined the knots. If she could just pull with her teeth, she'd be able to get free.

Little evidence remained from their work, only garbage and the single lantern nearby.

The ATVs started up. The smell of exhaust shot into the cavern. Rocks pelted against the walls of the entrance tunnel.

Jenny began to chew on the knot at her wrists and pulled as the rope loosened. Her body shook as the panic set in. She got her hands free, and then worked at the knots around her ankles. She kicked her way out the rest of the bindings.

She shuffled to the entrance, as feeling returned to her extremities. The noise of the machines faded in the distance. The shade hurt her eyes after so many hours of the cave's gloom, despite the lantern's light. She blinked and rubbed at her eyes. Pushing away at some bushes, she almost fell out of the entrance.

Freedom.

Between the rough terrain, and legs that didn't want to cooperate, she had to settle for a brisk walk. She kept a lookout for the men. She shook with a combination of fear, cold, and stiffness. *Down the hillside... just keep going...* Sliding on the thick layer of dry pine needles, she had to grab at things to keep from falling.

Someone yelled.

Terrified, she stopped to listen. Someone called out her name.

"I'm here! Help!" She screamed, scrambled, and slid in the direction of the voice.

"Jenny? Jenny, where are you?"

"I'm over here."

From the other direction, Mr. Shonee screamed his complaints about all the noise and racket. Jenny recognized his gruff voice.

That cute guy...Dean...from Sunday school ran towards her.

"Dean?" She ran towards him, slipping and stumbling the whole way.

"Oh my gosh, girl." He opened his arms. "Where have you been?"

She ran right into his arms and began to cry. "Some guys had me tied up in a cave."

"What?" He pushed her back, holding onto her shoulders. "Are you all right?" He looked at the dirty sweatshirt and her dusty jeans. "Did they hurt you?"

"It just hurts where the ropes were." She showed him raw wrists.

"Come on. We need to get you back to the ranch. Everyone's worried sick. Can you walk OK?"

"Yeah, I'm a little shaky, but I can walk. What are you doing here?" She was a mess. She raked fingers through her greasy hair trying to smooth it out. She cringed at the thought of what she must look like to this cute guy.

Dean put his arm around her shoulder to keep her steady as they walked. "Everybody has been out looking for you. The police, the forest rangers, the staff at camp. Even a bunch from church. Your parents are scared to death. I decided to walk around this way this morning."

"I didn't think I'd ever get out of there. I was so scared." She stifled a sob and leaned into him.

Barney came around the bend and ran towards them.

Mandy and Jon were on horses galloping to keep up with the dog.

"Jenny!" Mandy yelled. "Oh my gosh. Jenny. Dean, is she all right?"

Mandy's feet hit the ground before her horse completely stopped. She ran towards Jenny and threw her arms around the girl. "Are you all right? Are you hurt? Where have you been?"

Jon pulled a radio off his belt

"Some men had her." Dean. said. Holding Jenny's red wrists out. "They had her tied up in a cave."

"What? Who?" Jon's voice raised an octave as he placed his hand on Jenny's shoulder.

"That guy who works for you, Mark. I don't know who the other man was. I heard Mark call him Kane."

"They kept you tied up? What did they want? Are you hurt anywhere?" Jon stared at her, his eyes narrowing. "Did they…" He stopped.

"No." Jenny shook her head, tears in her eyes. "I'm fine. They didn't…they didn't…do anything. Just tied me up and wouldn't let me leave."

"Come on. We need to get you back to your folks. They're worried sick about you. You can fill us all in at the same time, but I'm getting the sheriff to meet us at the house. Jenny you get on with Mandy. Dean, hop on with me. Let's get her home."

"Wait." Jenny bent down and threw her arms around Barney's neck. "Oh, Barney. Thank you for being my friend."

Mandy knelt by her as tears welled up in her eyes. "I always knew I had a great dog."

17

Connie held her daughter like she would never let her go.

Rick had them both enveloped in his arms.

"I'm sorry," Jenny sobbed.

"Honey, it's not your fault. I'm just so glad you are back and safe with us." Connie ran her hand over Jenny's hair.

Rick walked over as the Sheriff approached. "You need to find the men who kidnapped my daughter. I want them arrested, now."

The sheriff held up a hand. "We'll get them. I need to talk to your daughter. We need as much information as we can get. Jon, there's more deputies on the way. Jenny, Jon told me some of what happened, do you think you can tell me the whole story?"

"Yes," Jenny said. "They didn't hurt me, except for tying the knots too tight. They just didn't want me to leave the cave. Well, Kane didn't. Mark…Mark was afraid of Kane and loosened the knots to help me."

Mandy motioned towards the picnic shelter near the cafeteria. "Let's all go sit down."

Sue came out of the office. "I radioed everyone, including the forest service, and told them she's been found safe."

"Thanks, Sue. Would you get us some lemonade and some food for Jenny?"

Everyone gathered around the picnic table under the shelter.

Jenny began the tale of her captivity. Connie sat next to her with a protective arm around her and held her close. Rick sat on the other side with his fingers tightly entwined. His knuckles were white.

Jenny had barely gotten into the story when Mr. Shonee tore into the parking lot. He spotted them and drove as close as he could to the shelter. A dust cloud enveloped the group.

Jon walked over to him.

The old man struggled out of his car, marched over and yelled, "Now y'uve gone and done it. You got them crazies out there lookin' for that girl and they drove right over my fence. You know what it takes for an old man like me to fix a dad-blame fence. What's the matter with you people? You're fixin' my fence, Phillips." A crooked finger pointed at Jon's face.

Jon held up his hands as the old man approached.

"Now listen, Shonee." The sheriff came over. "The girl is back, no one has been over there, yet."

"I know that. I seen her runnin' and that boy there, too." He pointed at Dean. "Just before that, some dad-blamed ATVs ran right over my fence across my back property. All the hollerin' and blasted noisy machines..."

"The two guys left on ATVs," Jenny said.

The sheriff grabbed his radio and gave instructions to the deputies to intercept the pair at the county road that ran to the west of Shonee's property. Within seconds, police sirens screamed past the ranch in that direction. "The deputies are heading over there to see if they can find them." He turned to Mr. Shonee. "We're just hearing the story from the girl about the men who held her captive in a cave."

"Well, I'd like to be hearin' that." Uninvited, the

old man hobbled over and sat down with the group. He hung his cane off the edge of the table, crossed his arms over his chest, and waited.

"Please continue, Jenny." The sheriff sat back down.

"That had to be the two men Mr. Shonee heard. Mark, and that other guy. They always came on ATVs. I heard them leaving as I untied myself, but I couldn't see right away when I got outside the cave so I didn't know exactly where they went. I just ran. Mark had loosened the ropes enough so I could get away. If he hadn't done that, I'd have been stuck there forever, unless Barney came back again. Mandy, he never left my side until I finally chased him off when I tried to run away, but they caught me before I could get out."

Connie gasped.

"Barney kept growling at those guys whenever they got near me. He kept me warm all last night. They made me work, but Barney just stayed next to me."

Rick's face grew more and more concerned. "What kind of work did they make you do?"

"Dad, you know that rodo stuff that that little boy showed you the other day?"

"Rhodochrosite?"

"Yeah, that stuff. They found a whole mess of it in that cave. I had to sort the red pieces away from the pink ones. I guess that other guy only cared about the dark red ones."

"Sheriff, if they found as high a quality as in that little piece the boy found, they could be pulling tens of thousands of dollars out of there. This area of Colorado has shown the richest veins in the country for rhodochrosite. The deep red Jenny mentioned is the most valuable."

Jenny told them how Mark had tried to be nice to her, but was clearly under the orders of the other man.

"We need to get up there and check this out. Did you get a name on the other guy?" The sheriff never looked up from writing down the details.

"Yeah, Mark called him Kane."

Mr. Shonee gasped, went pale, and gripped the table hard.

Jon reached out and grabbed the old man's arm. "Are you all right, Mr. Shonee?"

The old man's face wrinkled up even more and his voice faltered when he spoke. "What's this other guy look like?"

"Well, he was tall, like Jon. He had hair down below his ears but real messy and no style to it. Seemed like brown hair, but it was hard to tell in the dark cave. There were only a few lanterns and they kept them over where they worked."

"Did....did he have a mole above his left eyebrow? Deep voice?"

"Yeah, he did," Jenny hesitated. "How did you know?"

All eyes were now on the old man.

"Kane, you say."

"That's what Mark called him."

Shonee hung his head and slammed his fist on the table. "That's my good-for-nothin' son."

❧❧

Jenny sat behind Jon on an ATV and led the way to where the men held her captive.

Her dad, the sheriff, Dean, and Mandy rode on other machines.

Connie couldn't bear to see the place and stayed behind.

Barney ran along at about twenty feet or so off to the side and snooped around fallen trees.

Mandy struggled with the knowledge of all these endless new dangers on their property. "Lord," she began to pray. "This is really getting overwhelming. If I haven't thanked You enough yet for Jenny's safe return, I thank You again, now. I'm so relieved she's OK. Thank You for watching over her. Barney, too. Please help us figure out what these men are up to and where they are." Her ATV hit a rock and the front end jerked to the side. "And help me drive this thing better, Lord." she smiled. "In Jesus' precious name, Amen."

As they got closer to Mr. Shonee's property, Mandy worried for him. He had left without saying a word; a detective followed him to get a picture of Kane. It had to be difficult to learn his son could be capable of such deception, and then to actually keep a young girl captive...the old man had to be devastated. But with that hard shell he always put up, how would they ever reach out to him?

They made their way up the hill. Tire tracks in the earth headed straight over to Mr. Shonee's now downed fence.

Jon and the boys would be out here right away to repair it.

Jenny pointed up the hillside to an area that leveled out a bit before a sheer rock face. A lot of bushes were at the base of the hill.

Had Jenny found the right spot?

Jenny had Jon stop near a clump of brush. She hopped off and pulled at the bushes, revealing a large opening. An extensive cave went into the hill. All the brush hid the entrance from view.

The ATVs had emergency flashlights strapped to the rack so they had plenty of light to go into the cave.

"No one goes in except myself and Jenny," the sheriff said. "And don't touch anything out here until we get a team through here."

"Can't my dad and Mandy go with me?" Jenny's voice wobbled and tears filled her eyes.

The sheriff looked at the adults, and then nodded. "Jenny, it's a crime scene, so do not touch anything, you are simply leading us in to look around. Make sure nothing dangerous is going on."

Rick looked at the size of the opening. "There must be enough ventilation in here. Methane gas tends to be present in caves and mines, and can be deadly, but Jenny obviously didn't have any ill effects."

Jenny latched onto Mandy's arm and Mandy could feel her trembling. She slung an arm around the girl's shoulders.

They had to duck a bit as they made their way inside. They soon entered a larger open area.

Rick shone his light all around. "Oh my gosh…this is amazing."

Jenny pointed to the opposite side of the cave, her voice barely above a whisper. "That's where they kept me tied up. See the ropes?"

Mandy tightened her hold on the girl, pulled her closer and whispered, "It's OK now."

Rick walked over to the wall. "This cave most likely formed from high pressure water erosion leaving the sedimentary rock. It seems to be primarily calcium carbonate, or limestone. There is some dolomite here, too. Where these elements occur, rhodochrosite forms as the calcium carbonate rich water drips and forms. It looks like they found a low to medium hydrothermal vein of it along here." His face was near the wall of rock, fingers slightly in the air following the remains of the vein. "There are traces of the deep red color that signify minimal iron content."

Mandy, the sheriff, and Jenny looked at each other with raised eyebrows.

Rick looked around at the silent group. "Oh, um...conditions were right for the rhodochrosite to form. Apparently, they must have the more valuable specimens, making this all worth their while. No wonder they didn't want Jenny to get away.

"Do you know that rhodochrosite became the state mineral of Colorado in 2002?" No one replied, so he went on to explain, "During a study of rocks and minerals, John Ghist's Earth Science class from Platte Canyon High School near Bailey found that this state did not have an official mineral. Colorado has such a rich history of mining gold and minerals. They contacted State Representative Carl Miller and suggested rhodochrosite be named the state's mineral. He introduced legislation and less than three months later it received that designation.

"Colorado has such a translucent red variety in some areas that it is prized the world over. Some of it can bring tens of thousands of dollars, if the piece is large."

The sheriff had been listening intently, taking notes. "Well, we have our motive. Any idea how much they may have pulled out of here?"

"I sorted a lot from two big buckets." Jenny pointed to her spot.

"There's really no way to determine how much they got out of here at this point. The quality and clarity would be indicative of the value. To keep my daughter prisoner, they must have been finding a great deal of it. You need to find these men, Sheriff."

"Yes, we do. We'll have to check if there has been an influx of this mineral in the market, yet. I want everyone out of here now until we can get a team in to collect evidence. Thank you for showing this to us, Jenny. I know it has to be hard to be in this cave."

"You're welcome, but I want out, now." Jenny pulled on Mandy's arm, practically dragging her towards the entrance.

18

When they got back to the ranch, Mandy told Sue to contact the reporter and get a new story done on Jenny's return. Then she did some damage control to hang on to the remaining reservations.

Jon and Nate went up to repair the downed fence for Mr. Shonee. Nate couldn't believe it when he heard the whole story.

"No wonder Mark always seemed so distant around us. He was up to no good and probably didn't want to give anything away."

Jon removed the barb wire from the broken post. "Yeah, it's too bad we never got through to him. Maybe none of this would have happened."

Nate grabbed the new post strapped onto his ATV and carried it to where Jon worked. "Can't beat yourself up over that one, Jon. You did your best. You were real good to him. He was the one who betrayed you. Don't forget that."

"I know. I just hate to think what will happen to him now. He's a nice guy and still needs God. He helped Jenny escape."

"He also has to suffer the consequences. He made his decisions."

The two had the fence repaired quickly and headed back to the ranch.

The cave still had yellow police tape across the front area, and a team of investigators were going in and out of it with cameras and bags marked with the word "evidence" in their hands.

Jon hoped they would finish soon so they could eliminate yet another danger. He and Mandy had always thought it great to have an old mine on their property, but now he wondered if it was worth it. What else lurked on their land?

※

Mandy noticed the delightful smell of chocolate chip cookies. She asked the cook to bag up a dozen. She had to go see Mr. Shonee. The news of his son had to be tearing him up. She hoped the cookies would be a peace offering. She would ride Maggie.

Rick waved as she rode out of the corral.

Mr. Shonee was on his front porch in a chair leaning forward, hands resting on his cane. Weariness seemed to have aged the man even more.

She tied her horse to the rail by his garage and walked up to the house. "Hello, Mr. Shonee. I wanted to come by and see if you were all right."

He grunted. Moisture glistened in his eyes.

"I brought you some cookies. Chocolate chip." She waved the bag towards him.

"What do you want? You gonna gloat?"

She sat down and placed the bag of cookies on the small table next to him. "Jon and Nate fixed your fence." She dared to pat his hand. "Mr. Shonee, we care about you. You may not believe it, but we do. I came to make sure you were OK."

"You don't give a flip about me. We've never gotten along. Why should you care now?" His gruff exterior held its sharpness.

"We could get along fine if we just worked out our

differences instead of taking it to the extreme. We want to be good neighbors to you, Mr. Shonee. We really do. We'd like it so much if we could help you instead of you getting angry at us. God tells us to love our neighbors, and we do, it just...gets a little challenging, sometimes."

He finally looked at her, and he leaned back in his chair. "Me and God ain't been on speakin' terms for a long while." He reached for the bag next to his chair and took out a cookie.

"He loves you, you know."

Another grunt. He offered her a cookie.

She took it, hoping it was a tentative peace offering.

"No, I don't think so. God don't give a hoot about me. If he did, my rotten son wouldn't have turned out like this. I had to throw him out of here, ya know."

"No, I didn't know. Do you want to talk about it?"

"Nothin' to talk about. He expects me to give him everything he wants. He ain't ever held a job long enough to pay a bill. Sat around drinkin' and talkin' big, but never did nothin' about it. I got tired of takin' care of the lazy bum."

"I'm sorry. That had to have been hard."

"You know, I used to own part of your property. Sold it off. He always told me I was stupid for doing that."

"Yeah, I remember hearing that when we bought the place. There was an extra hundred acres to it, which is why we found it so attractive for our business."

"Yeah, that was mine. Just didn't see the need for it. My wife took sick and Kane did nothin' but bleed me dry. I needed the money. Dang near forty years old now, you'd think he'd grow up sometime."

Mandy took a moment to say a quiet prayer. "Kane has made his own decisions in life. God isn't going to force him to do anything. Kane has to want to do right. God isn't punishing you with your son's choices. God cares about you individually. He has to work on Kane separately."

"He's got a mighty big job ahead of Him."

Mandy laughed. "God has a mighty big job with all of us, don't you think?"

"Yeah, I reckon you're right about that. Guess maybe He done something today with you and me sittin' here eatin' cookies together."

"I think you're right. I'm rather enjoying myself."

The old man turned quiet. He shifted in his chair after a minute. "Yeah, I think I am, too."

They sat in silence for a time watching the trees move with the wind.

"How's that girl?"

"She's fine. I think she'll sleep for most of the day. Her scratches weren't deep so physically she'll heal up OK. She was pretty scared."

"Sure feel bad my own son did that to that family."

"I know," Mandy said. "He didn't hurt her, except for tying the ropes. He scared her, but he didn't do anything else."

There was a long silence.

Mr. Shonee finally broke it. "Want some coffee?"

"I'd love some."

"You want to go get it for us? I'm a bit slow goin' these days. Pot's on the counter, cups in the cupboard up above it."

"Sure, I'll get it. Take anything in it?"

"Black."

Mandy went in with a smile on her face. *The man is finally starting to open up.* "Lord," she whispered, "help me to reach him."

The small home was neat and tidy. Knick-knacks were sparse and the main furniture was from the 70's with its olive green tweed upholstery. Old brown shag carpet covered the floor. The home had an old musty smell to it. She went through to the kitchen, found the coffee cups, looped her finger through the handles and grabbed the pot. She went back out to the porch and poured him a cup.

"Thanks."

"You're welcome." She sat back down and drank from the cup she poured for herself.

"Gotta have coffee with cookies."

She smiled. "It's required." After a few more minutes, Mandy turned to him. "Maybe you'd like to come for dinner some time."

Another grunt.

"Come on. Wouldn't it be nice to get to know us more? Then we could talk things out. It's just dinner."

"Might be nice. Don't cook much for myself these days."

"How about tomorrow night? Six o'clock?"

"Fine."

Mr. Shonee grabbed another cookie as they finished their coffee listening to a Steller's jay squawk in a nearby tree.

19

Mandy rode back to the ranch with hope, and prayed this would be the start of a good friendship.

The clip-clop of Maggie's hooves lulled Mandy into a deeper state of peace.

The Carters were down at the pond. They talked and laughed together.

The horse whinnied, and the family turned to see her dismount. One of the teen wranglers came over and took care of Maggie. Mandy thanked him and brushed the dust from her jeans.

Jenny ran up to Mandy and hugged her. "Hi, Mandy."

"Hi, yourself. Did you get some rest?"

"Yeah, I took a good nap. My bed felt so good. Dad wanted us to leave, but I think I talked him out of it. I don't want to leave. I'm just not going to go out alone again. Ever."

Mandy laughed. "That's good. I don't want to look for you anymore. We need something else to do."

They both laughed as Rick and Connie joined them.

"Hey, Mandy." Rick seemed hesitant. "We want to thank you...and apologize. I'm sorry I got so angry at you and Jon. I know it wasn't your doing, but I was just so afraid of what may have happened to my little girl." He hooked his arm around Jenny's neck and pulled her in for a kiss on top of her head.

"I'm not little, Dad." She looked up at him and

grinned.

Mandy placed her hand on Rick's arm. "Don't give it another thought. We totally understand. I would have reacted the same way. Jenny tells me you're going to stick around for the remainder of your week. What would you think of a ride up into the mountains with Jon and me tomorrow morning? We'd like to give you some better memories than what you've had the last few days."

"Can we Dad, can we? Let's do it. That would be so much fun."

"Sure." Rick looked at Connie and grinned. "Let's do it. That's a good idea." After a few more minutes of small talk, they went back to their cabin.

Mandy looked up to the blue sky. "All things do work out for the glory of God and His good purpose."

Jon met her as she crossed the lot and gave her a hug. They headed to the office.

Apparently, all the excitement and adventures were appealing to some people. Mandy looked up from the registration book. "I hope there won't be any lasting ill feelings towards our place. Hopefully, memories of what Kane and Mark did here will soon be forgotten. We need to pray hard that they catch those two before they cause any more trouble."

They settled into their routine paperwork. The radio played calming inspirational music that soothed their souls and helped their attitudes.

❧

The receiver on top of the file cabinet crackled.

"We need help," a panicked voice screamed. "Is anyone there? Help!"

"This is base," Jon spoke in a calm tone, praying they had the means to help. "What's going on?"

"We've had a mountain lion attack. My buddy's hurt bad. We need help."

"Oh my gosh." Mandy jumped to her feet.

Sue picked up the phone and called 911.

Jon pressed the button on the side. "Where are you? Who is this?"

"This is Frank Wilson. Cabin number five. Ken brought us up here fishing the river. Sam made his way around a rock outcropping and got jumped by a lion. We had to beat it off with rocks and sticks. The lion is gone, but Sam is bleeding pretty bad."

"Ok, give me your location and we'll get help to you."

"Uh...I'm not sure what to tell you and Ken is trying to stop Sam's bleeding. We came quite a ways up the forest service roads. We are at a bend in the river. I'm looking at a sharp pointed mountain to the east. We've walked quite a ways from the Jeep."

Jon looked to the women and kept his thumb off the button of the mike, "They are too far from the Jeep to get us the GPS coordinates. At least he took the hand radio with him. Sue, pull up the topographic map. We have to try to pinpoint their location. Mandy get any available staff ready to head up. We have to find them. And tell them to take their rifles."

Jon turned back and keyed the mike, "Frank, listen, we're coming up. Tell me how far you think you went. Try to get Ken to tell you how far. And how serious is your buddy?"

"He's bleeding from his neck, head and arms. He's conscious, but fades in and out. Ken and Evan are applying pressure to the cuts, but he's in a bad way.

We came up about five miles and took a road off to the southeast. I think it showed a number 385 on one of those brown posts.... Yeah. Ken says that's right. What? OK, Ken says four miles up 385."

"We're on our way. Keep the pressure on his injuries. We've got medical on its way." Jon threw the hand mike back in its cradle.

"Sue, they're going to have to get a chopper up there. Call it back in. I think I know exactly where they are." Jon's finger traced the roads on the topographical map they kept in the office. He followed one of the forest service roads to the creek where they were probably fishing. The blue line on the map showed a sharp bend. "Here."

Mandy took note and called the dispatcher asking for emergency medical personnel and a helicopter.

Jon ran out the door.

At the barn, Tommy, Nate, and Phil had the Jeep Wagoneer loaded with the large medical bag, rifles and water. They tore out and headed up the forest service road out of camp.

Jon drove since he knew about where they were.

Nate navigated to make sure they didn't miss the turn-off for the forest service road marked 385.

They hadn't had any mountain lion issues in years and attacks were rare. However, the cats were opportunistic and one always had to be aware of that danger. If they were concentrating on the fishing, they probably didn't pay much attention to what might be behind them, or above them. Frank said Sam had just made his way alone around a rock outcropping. His movements must have enticed the cat to think he was prey.

Jon's heart pounded, and he prayed they'd get

there in time.

Nate leaned over and checked the odometer. "Should be about a mile more on our right."

Jon hit a rock that sent the vehicle up, and then slammed it back down. "Sorry." Nate pointed ahead. "The river should come into view soon, and then another two miles to the likely location."

Jon parked next to the other Jeep.

Tommy yanked the large red medical bag out, and flung it over his shoulder. Phil grabbed the backpack that he had loaded with bottles of water. It also held ropes and other miscellaneous things that could help in an emergency. All four grabbed a rifle. Jon took the walkie-talkie and they headed over to the river's edge.

Jon keyed the radio, calling Frank.

Static came over it then the frantic voice of the fisherman. "Yeah, are you close? We gotta get him some help. We spotted the lion again. It keeps pacing about fifty feet from us. It's gone again, but you better get here fast."

"We're almost to you. Hang on! Do what you can to look large, like pulling your jacket up above your head. Don't look the cat in the eye if it gets close, and whatever you do, don't run away." Jon looked over his shoulder. "Come on, guys. They've got more trouble."

Hollering could be heard above the sound of the rushing river.

Jon looked ahead and saw the men. One was throwing rocks towards the hillside. They could see the animal low to the ground and dodging the pelting rocks. The men were screaming at the lion.

Nate pulled the strap of his rifle around and grabbed the gun, leveling it in the direction of the cat. He fired off a shot well above the heads of the men, to scare the animal away.

The lion's feet jerked. It looked in the direction of the approaching men, let out a blood-curdling scream, and made another attempt at heading for the men by the water's edge.

Nate fired off another shot, which missed its mark, but did cause the cat to run off towards the trees. Nate was ready to fire again when the cat disappeared.

Jon made it to the injured man first.

Tommy lowered the heavy red medical bag onto the ground and began to unzip it.

Nate headed in the direction that the lion went to make sure it was gone. He fired one more shot into a tree near where the cat fled, just to ensure it kept going.

"How's he doing, Ken?" Jon knelt down to check the injuries.

Frank sat on the other side by his friend's knee.

"Tough shape. Glad you got here or we might have all been in tough shape." Ken kept his hands covering the bleeding gashes.

Jon took the offered pads from Tommy and used those to apply pressure to the worst of the wounds on Sam's head. Tommy checked the cuts on his arms that were thankfully superficial. Evan had a good hold on the worst one to lessen the bleeding. The deep scratches on Sam's neck were bleeding badly so more compresses were placed on those.

Nate took up the radio that lay next to Jon and called down to base. He checked his hand-held GPS unit and gave the coordinates.

Sue's voice crackled back over the radio. "Alpine Rescue is headed up."

It took a long ten minutes before the first

volunteers of the rescue team arrived with a litter to get the injured man to an area where the helicopter could pick him up.

"Keep the pressure on the wounds so he doesn't bleed out on us." Jon said, watching Alpine Rescue personnel as they came through the grasses.

The team loaded the injured man into a basket stretcher. Once strapped in, they carried their charge to their vehicle, and then rushed him to the meadow where the helicopter could land safely.

Jon knew they would take him to the trauma center in Denver.

Two forest rangers arrived on the scene and took notes of what had happened. The rangers, armed with high powered rifles, headed off into the forest to search for the big cat.

Jon and the guys helped get the distraught fishermen and gear up to the vehicles. Leaning on the hood of the Jeep, he drew them a crude map to show how to get to the hospital. "We'll get all your gear back to your cabin. It's going to be a long drive to the hospital, so be careful. Your cell phones will find a signal once you are back on the main road. Will you call us when you find out how he is?"

"Yeah, we will. Thanks for your help. We've got to head down there, now."

Ken stepped up to them. "I'll go with you. No sense trying to find the hospital on your own and you're in no condition to drive after all this." He got in the driver's seat without waiting for agreement from the men.

"Go. Stay in touch." Jon slapped the fender wall of the vehicle.

The three men drove off in the Jeep kicking up

rock and dust as they went.

The helicopter rose above the tree tops.

"Wow," Phil said. "Anyone remember the last time we heard a cougar attack around here?"

"I sure don't. There's got to be something wrong with that cat to attack like that," Tommy said.

Jon scanned the edge of the forest for any sign of the animal or the rangers. "Well, let's get back to camp. I've had enough excitement the last couple of days."

Jon radioed down to base to let them know they were on the way back.

"Jon," Sue's voice returned on the radio. "I was just going to call. We've got a problem here."

"What now?" Jon asked in exasperation.

"They spotted Kane and Mark in town. They were gassing up a truck when one of the deputies spotted them. They took off, but Jon, Kane had a gun and shot at the deputy. No one was hit, but the two could be headed back in this direction."

"Get everyone into lock down. Anyone outside, get to the cafeteria!"

"Already did, but Jon, Mandy and Jenny went for a ride on the horses and she doesn't have a radio."

"What?" Jon spun the four-door Jeep around so fast that the guys had to brace themselves to avoid slamming their heads into the side windows.

20

"Enjoying the ride?" Mandy turned back to Jenny.

They had left the ranch on horseback and headed west.

Barney ran alongside.

"It'll be quiet over this way now."

Connie had been hesitant to let her daughter go, but Jenny pleaded so hard, she relented.

The horses clip-clopped down the path in rhythm with each other at a gentle pace, calming nerves that had been on edge for too long.

"I hope everything is OK with that fisherman Jon went to help."

"The guys go out on several rescues every year." Mandy spoke over her shoulder. "It's not usually this serious. A fish hook in an arm or someone twists an ankle. Sometimes the rangers will call. We haven't had a call on a lion in a long time. Not a real likely thing to have happen, so don't worry about it. We're going the opposite way, anyway."

"As long as I'm with you and Barney, I know I'll be fine."

"I wanted to ride down this way and just peek over at Mr. Shonee's property. I hope he's all right. I feel so bad for him with what his son has done."

"I can't believe you'd care after all the trouble he gives you."

"Sometimes, Jenny, you just have to look beyond a person's actions and try to love them through God's eyes instead of your own. It's not always easy, but it's important to try."

"I prayed a lot in that cave."

"Did you?" Mandy turned quickly in the saddle, leather creaking.

"Yeah, I was so scared. I kept praying He would help me. It's weird how it made me feel better."

"That's the Holy Spirit holding on to you."

"The what?"

"Jesus promised us a Helper. The Holy Spirit's presence can get us through a lot of tough times. You just have to ask."

"I sure asked. I couldn't stop thinking they'd leave me there and no one would ever find me again. But Barney stayed with me."

"I know he's a great dog, but I'm still surprised he did that. He really likes you. I think God made sure you had a physical presence to know you were protected."

"It sure helped. I started thinking about what you and Jon said about Jesus being my friend and that He was with me always. Then there sat Barney keeping watch. It made me think that Jesus could be there, too. I felt a little better, then. Hey, there's Mr. Shonee in his yard."

He had his cane raised in the air, and he appeared to be yelling at someone or something.

"Let's tie the horses over behind that rocky area. Something doesn't feel right."

They got off their horses and tied them to the bushes by a large, boulder-strewn area. Mandy peeked around the rocks towards the man's property.

Jenny joined her.

"Barney, get over here," Mandy demanded in a

soft voice.

The dog obeyed, content to sit near her legs.

"There are some men walking from that shed in the back of his yard."

Jenny gasped and her hand flew to her mouth. "Mandy, that looks like Kane and Mark."

"Oh my. That is Mark, for sure. We've got to get the police. What are they doing there?"

The men were carrying boxes from the shed to the back porch area. Kane marched over to his father after he slammed the box down, and started to yell. Then he pushed the old man down into a chair.

Mandy's back went stiff, tension gripped her shoulders. "I should have brought my radio. Jenny, you get back to the ranch and have Sue call the sheriff. I'm staying here. I want to make sure Mr. Shonee isn't hurt."

"Mandy, no, come with me." Jenny's eyes were wide, fear etched deeply in her brow.

"Jenny," she grabbed the girl's arms and looked into her eyes. "You need to go get help. Barney, you go with Jenny. Go, honey. God will be with you."

The dog whined.

"Go, Jenny."

᷒᷑

The racing Jeep kicked up dirt as he pulled up to the building.

Sue came out of the office. "The police scanner said they have cars out searching for the men."

"Have Mandy and Jenny come back?"

"No, they haven't."

"Where did they go?"

"She said they were going to ride west, away from where the cat had been seen."

Jon ran towards the corral. The Jeep wouldn't make it far on the trail Mandy and Jenny had taken, so he had to take a horse. He mounted up and started towards the western trail.

Jenny came riding down the trail, the horse in a fast trot. "Jon," her voice rose, despite her being breathless. "Kane…Kane…and Mark are over at Mr. Shonee's. Mandy stayed to watch what they're doing."

"Go with Sue to call 911. Hurry." Then he kicked the horse's flanks and took off in a cloud of dust.

⁖

Kane continued his rough treatment of his father. He raised his hand as if to strike the old man.

Mandy got on her horse and hollered "Hee-ya!" The horse took off at a full run. She leaned forward and pulled back so the horse would jump the fence.

She raced near them hollering, "Get away from him." As she neared the back porch, she dismounted and ran to her neighbor's aid.

Kane leveled his gun straight at her.

She stopped in her tracks.

"What do you think you're doing?" he bellowed.

"What are you doing?" Mandy yelled back. "This is your father."

"You need to mind your own business. We just came for our stuff, and we'll be out of here."

Mandy ignored him, and turned to Mr. Shonee. "Are you all right?"

"Yeah, I'm OK. You shouldn't have come. Fool woman."

"I'm not going to watch you get hurt."

Kane laughed. "Yeah, and now you can both get hurt." He pointed the gun at his father. "None of this would have happened if you'd 'a just kept that property."

"Bah. Kane, you were bleedin' me dry. You're a lazy, good fer nothin' son. You could have just gotten a job and been responsible for yourself, but no, you had to leech off me all these years. I'm fed up with takin' care of you. What good was that land going to do for me, anyway?"

"Do you know how much money I been makin' out of that cave? It was ours, old man. I found that red gold when I was a boy, but I had no idea it would become so valuable. They got a big piece of it at the museum of the mining college that someone can have for a donation of ten grand. Ten grand! All that stuff in the cave was ours. You sold it off and I could have gotten that rock without all this trouble. If it weren't for Mark here, causing enough distractions to keep them people away from that side of the land, I may never have gotten in there."

Mark walked up from the shed carrying a duffle bag.

Mandy studied her former employee. "Mark. You started the fire, didn't you?"

He wouldn't look her in the eye.

"Yeah, but if he would have done it right, it would have been worse, and you'd have been too busy to work on anything else. Including nosing around the area." Kane shouted.

"And the note?" Mandy asked. "The brake line? You did that too, didn't you? How did you get involved with this guy?"

"We met in town a few years back. He thought if I got a job with you, we'd have a better chance of getting in that mine. Kane wanted the stones. He knew he had to get back in there. Said we could get rich." Mark stared at his shoes.

"Mark. We treated you like family."

"I know, Miss Mandy." He looked up, and then hung his head again. "I'm awful sorry it's come to this. I didn't want that girl hurt. She got away, didn't she?"

"Enough of this. You don't have to tell her nothin'. Shut up. I gotta think." Kane stepped over to the stuff they'd removed from the shed.

Jon called out to Mandy as his horse neared the fence.

Kane raised his gun and fired a shot high over Jon's head.

Jon reared up on the horse.

Mandy screamed. "Jon, go back."

"Listen to your lady, buddy. Get out of here or she's gonna get hurt."

Jon dropped down off the horse and stayed low. "Kane, the sheriff knows you're here. Let them go and you get out of here. The police are on their way."

Kane swore under his breath and glared at his reluctant partner. "Get them in the house. I'll get our stuff to the truck."

Mark motioned Mr. Shonee and Mandy inside.

Mandy helped Mr. Shonee get to his feet.

The old man whispered, "You shouldn't have come."

"We'll be OK. I've been praying hard. Help is coming."

❧❦

Kane continued threatening Jon with the gun even as he carried boxes to the truck that sat on the east side of the house. He dropped them into the back, and then went to the patio door. He yelled to Jon across the fence. "Get out of here man, or you'll be sorry. I'll kill her and the old man. You need to leave, now."

Terrified for Mandy, Jon offered a quick prayer. "God, protect Mandy and Mr. Shonee, please, I can't lose her..." He got on the horse and headed towards the ranch.

Kane went inside the house.

Once out of Kane's sight, Jon turned the horse and went towards the road. The deputies would arrive soon. He grabbed the radio and called in to Sue.

"Yeah, Jon. They're on their way. They should be there any minute."

"Call them and let them know Mandy and Mr. Shonee are being held hostage, now. I'm going to try and sneak over there."

"Jon, wait until help arrives. Let them handle it."

"Mandy's in there, Sue."

∂∞∞

Mandy and Mr. Shonee sat side by side on the old green couch in the living room.

Mr. Shonee pounded his cane against the floor. "Kane, for cryin' out loud. This is ridiculous. All this for money? You don't even care what happens to your old man. At least let Mandy go. You ain't got no reason to keep her here."

"Shut up. Since when do you care about them?" Kane went over to the front window, looked out, and then pulled the beige drapes closed. "If she'd minded her own business, she wouldn't be here."

Mark stood in the doorway of the kitchen, hands in his back pockets. "Kane, let's just leave. If we go now, we have a chance to get out of here."

Sirens screamed as the police raced down the road.

Kane began to panic. He locked the front door. "Lock the back door, Mark." He peeked through the drapes. "Dang it. There's two cop cars pulling in."

Mr. Shonee sat forward. His hands rested on the top of his cane.

Mandy gently rubbed his back to comfort the man as she stared down at her lap. Fear at how irrational Kane had become grew. Silently, she prayed.

Kane went to a small window on the other side of the front door and yelled to the approaching officers, "Get back or I'll shoot them both."

They must have done so because Kane began to pace.

Mandy pleaded, "Kane, just let us go. It doesn't have to get any worse."

Kane's red face deepened in color. "This is your fault." He grabbed her by the arm and pulled her to her feet.

She struggled to free herself.

Mr. Shonee swung his cane hard against his son's legs, which caused Kane to fall back.

Kane slapped the old man's face.

Mandy, furious that he would do that to his dad, pushed the unbalanced man.

Mark rushed over.

Kane grabbed at Mandy, but his grip fell away as she jerked back her arm. He still held the gun in his right hand. He fell on the floor, and then leveled the gun at Mandy.

She froze.

"No..." Mark hollered and flung himself at Kane.

Mandy fell towards Mr. Shonee, pushing him over on the couch.

A loud pop echoed in the room.

Mandy screamed.

Police burst through the door and were on top of the two men.

Mandy carefully moved off the old man.

Mark was bleeding and holding his arm. He had rolled away from Kane.

The police put handcuffs on Kane, who was pinned face down to the floor with an officer's knee in his back, arms behind him.

"Mark, are you OK?" She cried, searching for the source of the bleeding.

"Just go away, Miss Mandy." He rocked back and forth holding his arm, pain in his expression. He wouldn't meet her eyes.

"Mark, you took that bullet for me. Why would you do that?"

"I never wanted anyone to get hurt." He held his hand against the wound, but blood continued to drip between his fingers.

Two officers dragged a screaming and cursing Kane out the door.

A policeman came over to them, pressed the button on the microphone at his shoulder giving the all clear for medical personal to enter and began applying pressure to Mark's wound.

Jon burst through the door. "Mandy, are you all right?" Fear etched his face.

"Jon." She jumped up and threw her arms around

her husband. "I'm fine, but Mark's hurt."

"I thought you'd been shot." He buried his face into her neck and Mandy felt the warmth of tears.

"Mark jumped in front of Kane when he tried to shoot me." Her voice trembled as the adrenaline rush left her shaky. "He saved me, Jon."

The medics came in the front door with their large medical bags. One began to bind up Mark's wound. The other checked on Mr. Shonee, who abruptly waved them away.

"Mark, how did you get involved in all this?" Jon asked. "What were you thinking?"

"I didn't think anyone would get hurt, Jon. I've known Kane for a long time and we thought I could keep an eye on how much time you'd spend over by the cave that held the red gold. He said it was rightfully his, that he owned the land. I don't know, Jon. I'm stupid to get mixed up in this. I'm really sorry." He winced when the medics helped him to his feet to take him out to the ambulance.

The police escorted Mark and the EMTs to the waiting ambulance.

Mandy turned to their neighbor.

Mr. Shonee was leaning on the corner of the couch. A single tear ran down his face.

21

Mandy took Mr. Shonee's hand and guided him down on the couch. She sat next to him.

Jon squatted in front of him and placed a hand on his knee.

"Are you all right, Mr. Shonee?"

The old man sniffed. "What's the matter with that boy? I don't understand what could have made him do things like this. He could have killed any one of us. If he would have shot you, Mandy, I never would have been able to forgive myself."

Mandy leaned her head against the man's shoulder, and held his arm. "Even if he had, Mr. Shonee, it wouldn't have been your fault."

"He's my son! What did I do wrong with him?" Tears slid down his cheeks.

Jon patted the man's knee. "Mr. Shonee, Kane made his own choices in life. We can do all we can to lead our children right, but if they choose to go the wrong way, that's their decision."

"That's right. Remember when we talked that day on your porch? God can work on Kane, but He won't force Himself on your son. Kane chose wrong and has consequences to suffer, but it isn't your fault. We would never blame you."

"Why did you still seem concerned for Mark? He's just as guilty."

"Mark got caught up in greed and deceit. It explains a lot of why he's been so distant all these years. I've spent so much time praying for him to find Jesus, it's hard to just turn that off." Jon shook his head.

"You two seem to handle all this pretty darn good. You just ought to be really mad at me."

"Oh, Mr. Shonee, you're our neighbor." Mandy said. "I know we've had some tough disagreements, but we can't hold it against you. If we don't forgive you, how can we expect Christ to forgive us?"

"I don't know about that stuff. I just know you're different in how you react to this...to me." The man shook his head. "How will I ever forgive my own boy for all he did?"

"Only with God's grace in your heart, Mr. Shonee," Mandy said quietly. "We can do anything when we have Jesus in our hearts."

The deputy who stood in the doorway cleared his throat. "Um...sorry, I need to ask you all some questions."

Mandy really wanted to continue this conversation with her neighbor.

The deputy began asking questions about the entire incident.

Mr. Shonee raised his head. "I heard somethin' outside. I went to the back porch and saw Kane and that other young man out at my shed. It's quite a ways back there in the yard. My wife didn't like to keep things too close to the house. I yelled at them to get out of there. That's when Kane came marching up to the house yelling at me and Mandy showed up. I didn't even know they were hidin' stuff in the dang thing. I haven't used it in years. It's too hard for me to get back there."

"We're going through their truck," the deputy

said. "We'll get back to you if we have any other questions or information for you. Call if you think of anything else that may be important." The deputy set his card on the table and let himself out.

Mandy looked at the dark spot on the carpet and got up. "Do you have cleaners under your sink? We need to get that blood out of the carpet."

"Nah, just leave it. It don't matter none."

"Don't be silly. You don't want to see that every time you come in the room. I'm here, I can clean it. I don't think you want to get down there on your hands and knees to scrub it up."

"No, I don't 'spect I would. Rags and spot cleaner under the sink. Gloves, too."

Mandy found the needed items and set to work.

Jon helped her.

She sprayed the spot, scrubbed it hard, and worked the stain until it was gone. She prayed the whole time. She had a bucket of soapy water to rinse the rags in as they worked. Thankfully, the old brown shag carpet hid the remaining discoloration unless one knew where to look.

"Nope," Mr. Shonee said, as if he'd been thinking for a while. "Just don't understand you people."

Jon sat back on his heels. "What do you mean?"

"Just don't get why you'd be so nice to me after all that's happened."

"Like Mandy said, Mr. Shonee. We're God's children. If we expect forgiveness and love from our Lord, can we do less for our neighbors?" Jon asked.

"Well, I sure wish I could feel like that. Just don't rightly think God would want me."

"He does, Mr. Shonee. All you have to do is ask and believe." Mandy carried the supplies back to the kitchen. She continued to explain from around the corner. "God gave his only Son to die on the cross to save us from our sin. That's a lot of love."

Jon sat next to the man and looked him in the eye. "If you want, we can tell you more."

Mandy peeked around the corner in anticipation of his answer.

"Yeah, I think it's time I listened."

Mandy smiled. "I'll put on some coffee."

Jon looked around the room. "Do you have a Bible in the house?"

"The wife had one. I think it's over in the drawer of that hutch."

Jon had to struggle to get the old dark wood to open. Sure enough, under a lot of receipts, papers of all sizes, and some small tools, he found an old, well-worn Bible. "This was your wife's?"

"Yeah, she was a good woman. Died twenty-seven years ago. Cancer."

Mandy joined them. "I'm sorry to hear that. That must have been hard."

"Well, it's a good thing she wasn't around to see what our good for nothin' son turned out to be."

"There's always hope for him, Mr. Shonee. Have you ever heard the story of the Prodigal Son?"

"Nope."

Jon opened the book to Luke 15 and pointed to the passage. "Jesus told the story of a son who wanted his inheritance early so he could go off and live the life he wanted. He left home and lived a life of extravagance. He wasted it all with a lot of bad choices. It eventually left him with nothing. He had to take the lowest of jobs back then, feeding someone's pigs, and yet he was starving. He went back to his father who greeted him with love and acceptance. His father welcomed him back in, the past forgotten."

"You sayin' Kane will come back like that?"

"Not necessarily. He might, but the story really shows what all of us can be like. We all make bad choices. We all turn our backs on the Father. The heavenly Father."

Mandy continued, "And when we reach a point of realizing that God was right, we can turn back to Him, and He will accept us into His family. It's a heavenly party when we choose His Son, Jesus. God is like the father in the story. He wants us to return to Him. He's just waiting for us to ask. He'll welcome you back, right now."

"No matter what I've done wrong?" The old man's face held skepticism.

Jon smiled. "No matter what. We're all sinners, Mr. Shonee. We all needed Jesus to die for us so that we could receive eternal life in heaven. He not only died for us, He rose from the grave and waits for us to answer His knock on the door of our hearts."

"Sounds pretty simple. I've not been a nice man most of my life, as you know, and yer sayin' I can just ask and I'll get to heaven?"

"That's it." Mandy touched his arm. "You just have to believe in Jesus and what He did for us all."

"Considerin' my wife believed it, and she was a wonderful woman. Here you two are bein' nice to me, helpin' me, after what my son did to you. After all the trouble I've caused you over the years, and then you're scrubbin' my carpet. There's gotta be somethin' to this whole religion thing."

"It's not religion, Mr. Shonee," Jon said. "It's about a personal relationship with Jesus. Getting to know

Him as a friend. Just accept being a part of His family."

"We'd love to call you a brother in the Lord. Do you want that, Mr. Shonee?" Mandy searched the man's eyes.

"Yeah, I reckon I do. I sure need something to change in my life. It ain't been workin' the way I've wanted. I don't know how else I'm gonna get through this mess with Kane."

"We can lead you in a prayer. If you can truly believe that Jesus was God's son, sent to be a sacrifice for our sins, died on the cross and rose again, you can be called a child of God."

Mr. Shonee chuckled. "Ain't much of a child anymore, but I do believe what you say. It must be true."

Mandy sat next to him again.

Jon pulled up a chair and took the old man's hand and the hand of his wife. He explained, "I'll start praying, and then all you have to do is ask Jesus into your life."

"OK."

Jon bowed his head. Mr. Shonee followed his lead. Jon began, "Lord, we come to You today with thankful hearts. We thank You for protecting us through the difficult events of this day. We pray that You will watch over Mark with his injury and heal his wound. We especially pray that Mark and Kane will come to a realization that they, too, need You as their Savior.

"Lord, we now humbly bow before You as this man has made a decision to accept You into his life. Lord, we thank You for our neighbor, thank You for bringing us together today here in his home, that we might help him to know You. In Jesus' name. Go ahead Mr. Shonee. Just talk to Jesus. He's sitting here right now with us."

Mr. Shonee cleared his throat, and in a raspy, shaky voice, he began. "Well, Jesus, I can see I really need You in my life. Never thought much before about it, but I can see it now." He whispered to Jon, "What else do I say?"

"Just say what you believe about Him."

"Well, I um…I believe what Jon and Mandy have told me today about You bein' God's Son and all. My dear wife Betty tried to tell me for years. I just been too stubborn to listen back then. Then I just been mad at You for taking her away. But now I see. I believe that You even died for an old codger like me. I've been pretty awful all these years. Don't want to be that way no more. I'm tired. I believe You do love me. I know there's something different and better in folks who believe in you. I want to be different, too. I believe You rose up out of that grave and Yer just waitin' for me to ask. So Lord, I'm askin'. Help me to change and to know You. Um…in Jesus' name."

Mandy couldn't focus through the tears in her eyes.

"Was that right?" Mr. Shonee asked.

"It's always right when someone asks for Jesus to come into their heart." Jon smiled.

"Oh, Mr. Shonee." Mandy threw her arms around the old man and cried tears of joy.

Mr. Shonee laughed and patted her back. "You women cry at everything."

Mandy laughed and pulled back. "I'm so happy for you, Mr. Shonee. Welcome to the family!"

"Well, thanks. Guess I got me some learnin' to do now. You think an old codger like me can learn this stuff?"

Jon opened the Bible to the book of John. "This is a good place to start. I'll put a book mark here and you read this when you can. It'll tell a lot about Jesus and His life. It'll also give a lot more information on what He did for us on the cross. But I want to show you, here in chapter one, verse fourteen. 'The Word became flesh and made His dwelling among us. We have seen His glory, the glory of the One and Only, who came from the Father, full of grace and truth.' Jesus came as a man to offer Himself as a sacrifice because He's the only one who could remove the sin of mankind for payment of sin. Jesus is the beginning, so the more you learn about Him, the more you'll understand and grow to love Him. Just read."

"OK, thanks. I'll do that."

Mandy added, "You can always call us, too, with questions you may have. You could also join us for church, sometime."

The man's countenance seemed to be changing before their eyes. "I think I'd like that."

Jon stood. "We better get back to the ranch. Sue's going to want more details."

"Oh my gosh," Mandy exclaimed. "You're right. We better go. Can we do anything else for you before we leave, Mr. Shonee?"

"Nah, go on. Your day's been messed up long enough." Mr. Shonee attempted to get up. Jon took his arm and helped him rise. The three exchanged hugs.

"You call us if you need anything, OK? And don't forget, dinner tomorrow night at our house," Mandy said on her way out the door.

"I'll be there. Thanks for…everything."

"You bet. Bye." Jon waved.

22

Sue met them at the office door. The deputy had stopped by to fill her in.

They apologized for the delay and filled in the details.

Sue cried as she heard about Mr. Shonee's acceptance of Christ. "I should have known you'd be out there ministering. I'm so glad everything worked out so well today."

"God promises and He fulfills. I'm heading down to the barn and the shop to check on things." Jon walked out the door.

Mandy practically fell into the chair by Sue's desk.

"Tired?"

"Tired and hungry. If this is any indication of the rest of the summer, I don't know how we'll make it."

"Yeah, this has been a bit much. We got a call from Frank at the hospital. They got Sam patched up, but they'll have to watch for infection. He lost a lot of blood, but they think he'll pull through."

"Any word from the rangers on that cat?"

"No, nothing yet. I've let all the guests know to be extra careful and stay together if they go up the trails."

Jenny suddenly burst into the office. "Mandy, you're OK." She threw her arms around Mandy's neck, almost knocking her over.

Mandy laughed and hugged her back. "I'm fine. Everything is good. They have Mark and Kane in custody. Mark got shot though, but he's going to be fine."

"Who shot Mark?"

"Kane was going to shoot Mandy, and Mark threw himself in the way," Sue answered.

"Oh, Mandy..." Jenny dramatically hugged her friend.

"It's OK, Jenny. Everything's over with now. Come on. Let's go for a walk."

"Oh, my dad wants to talk to you."

"Well, let's go find him."

They walked out of the office and found Jon and Rick talking in the parking lot.

Jon looked at them. "Mandy, come here a minute. Rick has some interesting news." A huge smile lit Jon's face.

"Do I dare ask?"

"Well, as you know, I'm a geologist," Rick said. "The discovery of the rhodochrosite here is a real treat. My company often takes on projects like this when a discovery is made of minerals of interest or value. We'd like to explore the possibility of more specimens in that cave. Of course, it's purely study on our part. Any further wealth would go to you since you own the property."

"Wow. You think it is worth more exploration?"

"Oh, definitely. There's just one other thing. Jenny, we'd have to spend the summer here."

"Really, Dad? Can we really?" Jenny grabbed his arm.

Rick laughed. "Well, it's up to the Phillips's here if they want us around and if they agree to the further exploration. And I guess if they want to put up with us all summer."

Jon and Mandy looked at each other and grinned.

Jon reached out his hand to shake. "I think it would be great to have you stay. Whatever you find up there would be quite interesting. Can you really work that out with your job?"

"Oh, yeah. That *is* my job. And it's my company."

"Well, let's head over to the office and you and I can discuss this in more detail. We'll have to check in with the sheriff and get the all clear. And after all this, the cabin is on us." Jon slapped Rick on the back. They headed off together.

Jenny jumped up and down, squealing with excitement. "Wow. I get to spend all summer here. This is so great."

Mandy hugged Jenny. "It will be wonderful to have you and your family around. But please, no more need to be rescued, OK?"

Jenny laughed. "I promise I won't go anywhere alone."

❧

Jenny skipped off to tell her mom the news.

Mandy went to the barn to talk to Nate. She found Nate and Phil repairing one wall where a horse kicked a hole during a cranky moment. "Hey, guys. What's up?"

"Hey, Miss Mandy. Just fixing what a horse set out to bust up."

"Well, now that everything has settled down a bit, we need to get to work on the town site. Nate, can you call the contractor in the morning and get him started?"

"Sure, Miss Mandy. I'll take care of it. We're about done here."

"Thanks, Nate. I'm so excited." She turned and went off to get some dinner. Bedtime would not come fast enough tonight.

❧

Jon and Mandy finally got into the house around nine.

Mandy yawned and stretched.

Barney curled up by the fireplace on his big dog pillow.

A cool breeze blew through the windows.

Jon pulled off his jacket. "I'm exhausted. This one day feels like three."

Mandy slouched down onto the couch.

Jon sat next to her and wrapped his arm around her shoulders.

She leaned in. "I know. What a day. Who would have thought this morning that we'd have a day like that?"

Jon pulled her closer. "Are you doing all right? You had a pretty harrowing time over at Mr. Shonee's."

She yawned again. "Yeah. I'm OK. I'm just so thankful that even through all the bad things that happened over there, he was willing to give his heart to Jesus. Oh Jon, wasn't that wonderful? I still get chills when I think about it. God is so good!"

"Funny how the Lord works, but He sure was working overtime over there today."

"I asked Nate to call the contractor in the morning to get things started on the town site. I sure hope life can get back to normal now so all of that can proceed."

"I had the same thought. Thanks for getting Nate

on it. At least the ground is leveled and ready. They can start forming the slabs and by next week the buildings should be able to be constructed."

"It's finally happening, Jon. I can't wait to have them finished and get in there to decorate them. Maybe Jenny can help me since they'll be around this summer." Mandy's excitement bubbled to the surface. She sat forward and looked at her husband. "Oh, then we could set up the little store together. Maybe she'd even like to run it later this summer."

Jon pulled her back against him and wrapped both arms around her tight. "Shhhh...settle down. It's bedtime, and you'll get all riled up again."

Mandy laughed as she looked up at his face.

His eyes closed.

"OK." She sighed. "I guess I have to be patient again. Let's go to bed. I am not going to be able to carry you up."

"In a minute. I like it here." They nestled into the couch. Soon, light snores came from her husband.

She thanked God for His part in saving them that day, and then closed her eyes as she snuggled against his chest.

23

Jon and Mandy prepared to take the Carter family into the mountains for the day. They packed a cooler with sandwiches and water bottles.

Mandy put a large roast with potatoes in the slow cooker remembering that they'd also invited Mr. Shonee for dinner. "Lord, You cook this roast for me today since I'll be busy," she murmured with a grin and headed for the door.

Jon pulled up in a Jeep.

Jenny and her parents walked over from their cabin.

"Good morning," Mandy said. "Are you all ready?"

Rick had his arm around his daughter's shoulder. "We sure are. We've got our hiking boots, hats, and sunscreen. We're ready."

Jenny had her hair in a high pony tail and pulled through the opening in the back of her pink baseball cap. She wore denim, knee length shorts with a purple and pink plaid shirt. "Where are we going today?"

"Thought we'd take you up to the high country and hike around close to tree line," Jon replied. "It depends on how much snow is left. We could see some mountain goats. Could be some babies running around now, although it's a little early for them. Got your cameras?"

Connie held up her camera. "Yes we do. I would love to see some wildlife, just no mountain lions."

"Well, let's go. Rick, you sit up front with Jon. Us girls will fit in the backseat better." Mandy headed to the door.

"I get the middle," Jenny said diving in.

Connie laughed. "Well, I won't fit well in the middle anyway."

Jon headed out to the main road to go west up to the high mountain pass. He pointed. "We'll be there soon. I think you'll really like the views up this way." He turned the vehicle to the left to take a steep, dirt road. The forest changed from the thick Ponderosa pines to the smaller lodge pole pines. That tell-tale reddish brown color tinged the forest in many areas, but hadn't completely taken over, yet. Snow lay in the shady areas. Small fingers of water ran down the side of the road causing a slight rut to form in the ditch.

"Oh, look at the river." Jenny pointed out the window.

"This is Jackson creek. I think we'll pull over here for a minute. This is a beautiful spot for a family photo."

"A family photo is a great idea," Connie said. We could use that for our Christmas card this year."

"There's a huge boulder right down there you could all sit on with the creek behind you. The water is running high with the spring run-off. It was a mild winter, but it's still running pretty good." Mandy led the way.

The group made their way to the creek sliding a bit in the loose pebbly rock that covered the small hillside. The water roared loud enough that they had to yell above the sound.

Rick hopped on the boulder that Mandy pointed to. He reached out a hand to his wife and daughter.

Jon stayed on the bank with the camera to get a good shot of them and the creek beyond.

"There, got it." Jon hit the review button on the digital camera. "Hang on. I'm going to get one more angle." He stepped to his left, trying to avoid slipping on the rocks. He planted his foot against a clump of grass and took another shot with them off to the side with the roaring water beyond. "Beautiful."

Everyone turned to look at the rushing water. A cool misty breeze blew towards them, which felt good with the sun bearing down. After a few more minutes, they all made their way back to the Jeep.

Jon headed to the first switchback. After several more, he pulled off on a very wide area.

"Oh my gosh," Rick murmured.

Mandy opened her door and stepped out. "Come on. You need to see this."

They all gathered by the guard wall built out of mortared rock. The view down the canyon they had just come up was amazing. Trees as far as one could see. Pines, aspens, some reddish brown mixed in, they also saw a lake in the distance reflecting the sharp blue of the sky.

"Wow," Connie said quietly.

Jenny sat on the wall and swung her legs over the side, startling her mom, who grabbed her shoulder.

"Oh, Mom, I'm fine."

"Be careful, Jenny. That's a long ways down."

"I know. I'm being careful."

Rick took lots of photos before they once again loaded into the Jeep.

When the vehicle made its last turn on the mountain, it finally opened into a high meadow. Not many pine trees grew there. The short vegetation grew in patches against the pebbles and sand.

Jon made a turn at a brown forest service sign that indicated the trail head. He parked, and they all got out. One other SUV sat empty in the small lot.

"Grab your water bottles. At this altitude, you'll need to stay hydrated. We'll go slow, but drink before you are thirsty. Altitude sickness is just not fun. If any of you start feeling a bad headache, we'll have to go down to a lower elevation. But if you drink enough water, you'll be OK."

"What elevation are we at here?" Rick asked as he hooked his water bottle holder to his belt loop.

Jon checked his GPS unit before he clipped it to his belt. "We're at 10,100 feet." He flung a small backpack onto his shoulder.

Mandy slipped into her jacket. "Grab yours. You're going to want them out there. The winds pick up fast sometimes."

"It's cold up here. There's still snow on the ground." Jenny ran laughing to a large snow-covered area. She made a snowball and lobbed it at her dad. He made his own, and tossed it at her. She turned her back to him and it splattered against her backside. They both laughed as Rick grabbed her around the waist spinning her in a circle.

Mandy chuckled. "You're going to wear out before we hit the trail."

Rick struggled for a breath. "Wow. The air really is thin up here isn't it?"

"That it is. Come on. Let's head up a ways." Jon led the way to the trail.

Jenny shivered. "I should have worn my jeans."

"Seems to me I mentioned that this morning," Connie chided.

The adults walked around the snow, while Jenny stomped right through it laughing.

Once through the denser part of the twisted trees, the view opened up to a meadow.

"Look." Jenny pointed to where several white furry animals with short black horns grazed about half a mile away.

"That's the mountain goats. See if there are babies," Jon said.

A couple of the goats looked in their direction, and then went back to feeding on the new grass. Two very small, fuzzy babies suddenly appeared romping around the legs of a larger animal whose thicker fur showed the molting stage.

Connie exclaimed, "Oh, my. Babies."

"Aren't they cute?" Mandy said. "This is exciting. First babies of the season. I'm so glad you got to see them."

Jon checked his watch. "Do you want to watch more or should we move on?"

"I'd like to experience it all," Connie replied, even as she looked back at the babies. She turned to Rick and Jenny, who nodded in confirmation.

Rick tripped on a rock in the path. "My legs feel heavy and wobbly."

"That's the altitude. Just take it slow." Jon moved to walk beside him.

A cold wind blew at their faces. Very dark clouds were coming up and over the mountain ahead.

"Oh, boy." Jon stopped. "We need to go back to the car. That cloud does not look good."

"Oh, you're right," Mandy agreed. "Let's head on back."

"Ahhhh, why do we have to go back? It's just a

cloud." Jenny gave a pleading look.

"When you are this high in elevation, storms can come up fast and furious." Jon's voice was firm. "We are sitting ducks out here with so few trees. We'll just be safer if we get back to the car."

A bolt of lightning hit the nearest peak followed by a roll of thunder.

They all jumped.

"I can't believe how fast that moved in. It's much colder all of a sudden." Connie rubbed her arms, despite the jacket.

Another sudden flash caused them all to duck. The engulfing sound of thunder echoed across the mountain tops.

Instinct made them all start running. Fog rolled in and the mist inside the cloud dampened already chilled skin. Low rolling thunder continued to resonate.

"Button your jackets and pull your hoods up." Mandy commanded as hard rain drops slapped down.

Rick hollered out, "I've never seen anything like this."

"I know." Jon began to run. "Everyone get to the car."

Jenny didn't need any further prodding. Her long, slender legs got her ahead of the others as she bounced around the obstacles in the path.

Another bolt cracked off the mountain.

Jenny dropped to the ground.

The adults caught up to her, and Rick pulled his daughter to her feet.

"It sounded like it was right on top of me," Jenny's tone was breathless. "It scared me."

They piled into the car, gasping for breath.

Jon turned the heat on as soon as he started the car. The windshield fogged up. He let the engine idle, waiting for it to clear.

"That's the worst storm I've ever experienced," Rick said.

"Mountain storms come up fast. You have to be ready every time you go out since the weather can change in a heartbeat at these elevations. A lot of people get caught unprepared." Jon flicked on the headlights.

"What's that?" Jenny shouted, pointing out the window.

Jon wiped at the still foggy windshield.

Two people were attempting to make it back to their car. The large man had his arm over the shoulder of the woman, and he was limping.

Rick and Jon looked at each other.

"Let's go." Rick nodded at Jon.

They jumped out of the car.

"Be careful," Connie yelled, just as the door shut.

The guys each raised one arm of the limping man onto their shoulders. The woman ran ahead and unlocked the car doors. They lowered the man into the passenger seat and lifted his injured leg up into the car. Jon and Rick got the door shut, waved to the couple and ran back. A rush of cold wet air gushed in as they tumbled into the Jeep.

Mandy asked, "Is he all right?"

"Yeah, twisted his ankle at that last loud crack." Jon replied. "He's pretty sure it's just a sprain."

"The wife is going to take him to get it checked." Rick shook his shoulders to rid the jacket of water.

Jon shifted the Jeep into gear. "Well, I believe that ends our trip to the mountain tops today. I think we'll head back down where the weather will be better."

"I think that's a good idea." Connie snuggled against her daughter. "We'll have all summer to explore places like this."

"I want to come back and see those goats again." Jenny grinned as she cuddled into her mother.

❧⚮❧

The weather did improve further down. Dark storm clouds lingered on the mountain top.

"Let's head to the picnic area by the lake, " Mandy suggested.

The picturesque spot by the lake had pine tree covered hills, and gray snow-capped mountains behind making the scene perfect for photos. Ducks floated on the water, occasionally ducking below the surface and popping back up.

Connie and Mandy covered the old wooden picnic table with a plastic tablecloth and set out the food. The sun warmed their soggy clothing. They heard a loud squawking in the trees around them.

"What on earth is that?" Connie searched the trees.

"Oh, that's just the camp robbers. They'll be down here any minute looking for a handout."

"A camp robber?" Jenny's gaze showed alarm.

"A Gray Jay," Jon put a hand on her shoulder. "They'll come steal food right off the table if they think they can get away with it."

Rick laughed as one landed a few feet away from the table.

The bird's body was gray, but parts of its head were white with a half cap of black. The bird showed no fear of his human audience

"Well, we have a guest for lunch today." Connie clicked her tongue at the bird.

It hopped forward looking for a snack.

They all settled around the table making their sandwiches and passing chips.

Mandy set a bag of grapes in the middle. The jay kept trying to land on the table, but Mandy shooed it away.

"And you live here." Rick looked around and sighed.

"Yeah, there's a saying around here, 'If you're lucky enough to live in the mountains, you're lucky enough.'" Jon grinned. He and Rick wandered off, then sat down in the grass, talking.

"It just encourages people to get to know one another, being out here," Connie said as she glanced at the men.

"That it does." Mandy smiled, glad her guests were appreciative of the serenity.

24

As the afternoon waned, they headed back to the ranch.

Jon pointed out all the interesting sights as they went.

Connie yawned so often she had to apologize.

"Going up in the elevation always causes me to feel sleepy," Mandy said, and then yawned, too.

Connie's head leaned against the headrest, and she fell sound asleep.

A comfortable silence descended as Jon drove.

"Hey, what's Mr. Shonee doing laying in the yard?" Jenny's voice jolted everyone.

Jon slowed to turn in the driveway.

Mr. Shonee was near the driveway in the sparse grass. Scattered mail fluttered all around him, his cane just out of reach. He clutched his chest in obvious distress.

Jon jumped out of the car and ran.

Mandy moved just as fast.

Jon knelt down beside him. "Mr. Shonee, are you all right? What happened?" He began to loosen the buttons on the man's shirt collar.

Mandy took his hand in hers. "Mr. Shonee..." She choked on the rest of the words.

The old man struggled to get air into his lungs. "Jon...Mandy...it...feels...like...someone's...
standing...on my chest." He gasped for breath.

Jon looked back at Rick. "Go in the house and call

911. Then call the ranch and tell Sue what's going on."

"Right." He ran inside and returned with a small pillow and a blanket; he continued to tell the dispatcher the situation.

"It hurts so bad...s-scared," Mr. Shonee choked out.

"Pray, Mr. Shonee. We're all here. We're going to help you," Mandy said, continuing to stroke his arm.

His eyes glistened as he looked up at her. He gasped and clutched his chest. The color of his face turned dark red, and then went to a deep blue color as he went limp.

Connie grabbed Jenny and took her to the car. They both cried and held on to each other, eyes wide with concern.

Rick still held the phone to his ear.

Jon checked for a pulse. "Nothing," he said. "No pulse, I'm starting compressions." He ripped open the man's shirt and began frantically pumping his chest.

Mandy sobbed, but kept Mr. Shonee's chin positioned while Jon worked. She mumbled a constant prayer for the Lord to bring him back.

"You need to hurry," Rick spoke with the dispatcher. "The ambulance is on its way." He said to Jon and Mandy.

"Come on, come on...you can do it, Mr. Shonee. Come on..." Jon huffed out the words.

The sirens screamed towards them.

Rick went out on the road and waved the ambulance in. He then placed a call to High Country Safaris to let them know what had happened.

The sheriff also arrived.

Nate and Sue drove up.

The medics jumped out, got their gear and the

gurney out of the back of the vehicle. The driver spoke into the radio attached to his shoulder strap. "Unit One. On scene with two people doing CPR on an elderly man."

"We've been doing CPR for three minutes." Jon didn't look up.

One medic nodded and began to hook up the leads for the monitor.

The other medic immediately got the oxygen hooked up to the bag-valve mask and placed it on Mr. Shonee. He turned to Mandy. "Do you know how to do this?"

"Yes." She squeezed the bag.

Mr. Shonee's facial color changed from a blue ashen appearance to pink.

Nate and Sue stood off to the side, held hands and bowed their heads, silently covering the scene with more prayers.

Once all the leads were in place, the medic said, "Stop CPR." He watched the monitor. "Patient's heart is in fibrillation. I'm getting the paddles. Resume compressions." Jon began the process again.

The paramedic had the paddles ready in seconds. "Clear!"

Jon sat back on his heels, arms raised, and Mandy lifted the oxygen bag away.

The medic delivered the defibrillation shock. Mr. Shonee's body thrust up and his back arched for a split second. The medic then checked the monitor. "Check for breathing."

Mandy leaned over, and then sat up. "He took a breath."

"Jon, switch to the non-re-breather mask." The medic handed Jon the new mask and then took over.

They readied Mr. Shonee for the trip in the ambulance.

Jon scooted to the side and worked to catch his breath.

Nate walked over and put a hand on his shoulder. "Good job," his friend whispered.

Mandy stood, feeling shaky.

Sue's arm wrapped around her waist. "Trust the Lord, Mandy. Trust the Lord."

The sheriff pulled out his notepad. "You OK, Jon?"

"Yeah, Ed. I'll be fine."

"How did you find him?"

Jon stood brushing the back of his jeans and relayed the story of driving by when Jenny saw him lying out in the yard.

"No other family, is there?"

"No, Kane is it, and I doubt he cares right now."

"Right. OK, I'll check in at the hospital later."

"Thanks, Ed." Jon noticed Mandy, and he grabbed her up in a tight embrace.

"Jon, he just has to make it," Mandy spoke, but tears clogged her voice. "We just made peace with each other. I want to get to know him."

Nate and Sue gathered close with a hand on each of them. Nate said, "Let's all pray right now. Rick, you want to join us?"

Connie and Jenny walked over to the group.

Jenny grabbed hands as they formed a circle to pray.

Nate led a passionate, heart-felt prayer.

The presence of the Holy Spirit comforted Mandy as she listened.

25

Sue handed Jon her keys. "Mandy, Jon, take my car and follow them to the hospital. Nate and I will go back to the ranch in the Jeep with the Carters. Just call and keep us posted. I'll contact the church and get more prayers going for him."

"Thanks Sue," Jon said. "We'll phone in a while. Come on, Mandy. Let's go be with him."

They got in the car and made the somber, quiet drive into town.

Mandy could only stare out the side window praying constantly that their neighbor would pull through. At least, his heart was beating again. "Surely that's a good sign, Lord." Her words were loud enough for Jon to hear.

He reached over, took her hand, and squeezed it. "We have to give him to Jesus, Mandy. He belongs to Him now. We have to hang on to our faith that either way, he'll be fine."

"I know." She lowered her head. "I just pray we have the chance to get to know the real man, now."

They pulled into the parking lot and rushed inside.

"We're here to see Mr. Shonee," Mandy said to the nurse.

"Are you related?"

"We're his neighbors."

"I'm sorry, but only family can see him or get any information about him."

"But...we're the ones who found him." Mandy's back went straight, ire building.

"I'm sorry, but that's the rules. There are privacy issues."

Jon placed a hand on Mandy's arm. "He has no family. There is no one else to be with him."

The nurse now looked genuinely sorry. "I wish I could help you, but I can't."

Just then, Sheriff Ed walked in. "Hey Jon, Mandy. How is he? I wanted to come by and check on him and the two of you."

"We don't know." Mandy turned and leaned against the counter. "We're not allowed to see him."

Ed turned to the nurse. "Get one of the doctors out here, please."

Without a word, she walked through the swinging doors. She returned moments later with a tall man in blue scrubs. He seemed very rushed and impatient.

Ed came over to the man. "Doctor, this couple is the only family Mr. Albert Shonee has. I recently arrested the man's son. They need permission to see him. They were the ones who kept him alive with CPR to get him here."

The doctor's face showed frustration. "All right, on the sheriff's word, you are now family. Nurse, they're allowed, but only one of you can come back at a time."

Jon gently pushed against Mandy's back. "Mandy, you go. I'll be right out here. Thanks, Ed."

"I never even knew his first name." Mandy whispered to the two men.

The nurse motioned for Mandy to follow.

Mr. Shonee lay in the bed, eyes closed, an IV tube in his arm, wires coming off his chest to a beeping machine, and an oxygen mask on his face. He still looked so weak, so vulnerable.

A different doctor stood near the bed writing information on Mr. Shonee's chart. The nurse introduced her as family, so the doctor began telling her what had happened.

"From what we have learned so far, he has a minor blockage in one of the arteries in his heart. We have him on blood thinners and some pain meds. He should regain consciousness soon. He's a very fortunate man for his age. I understand CPR was started immediately?"

"Yes. My husband and I found him before he..." she choked on the word. "We started CPR right away."

"Well, that will be a major help to his recovery. Time is of the essence when this happens. Since he had help right away, he shouldn't have suffered oxygen deprivation, so that will also benefit him. I'll check back in a little while." The doctor left tugging the curtain around the track for privacy.

"Thank you, doctor."

She pulled a chair near the bed and sat down. She took Mr. Shonee's hand in hers and began to pray. Then she felt a little twitch in his hand. She looked up to see his eyelids fluttering a bit.

"Mr. Shonee?"

The man groaned, and his eyes blinked. "Mandy? Where...?" He scanned the surroundings and fumbled to remove the mask.

"Don't take the mask off. It's OK, Mr. Shonee. You're in the hospital, but you're going to be all right."

"Who hit me in the chest?" he asked as he rubbed his ribs. His first finger had an oxygen sensor on it, and he raised it to look at it. "What's happened here?"

A nurse came through the curtain. "Hello, Mr. Shonee. How are you feeling?"

"I feel like a truck hit me. What in tarnation is goin' on?"

"He's about back to normal," Mandy murmured.

The nurse smiled as she checked his vitals. "I'm going to go get your doctor, now."

"I ain't deaf, for cryin' out loud. She don't have to yell like that."

"You sure scared us. Do you remember what happened at all?"

"I went out to get the mail." He hesitated, as if in search of something. "Hadn't been feeling too good all day."

"We found you lying near your driveway."

"I think I remember seein' you. Did I—"

The doctor pulled the curtain open. "Welcome back, Mr. Shonee." The doctor reached out to shake the old man's hand.

"Doc. What happened to me?"

"You experienced a myocardial infarction."

"A what?"

"A mild heart attack, Mr. Shonee. But your family found you right away and did CPR on you and brought you back."

He looked at Mandy. "You two did that?"

"Well, we couldn't just leave you lying there." Mandy smiled.

"I'll be…"

The doctor continued, "We're going to have to do a procedure called angioplasty, but I don't foresee any complications as long as you behave yourself. You're going to be with us for a few days, maybe a week."

"I don't need that. My chest just hurts a little. Send

me on home." His gruffness had returned.

"Oh, no, you don't." Mandy put a hand on his shoulder. "With as hard as I've been praying, you're going to do what the doctor says."

"You should be able to get out of here in a week, but you are not going to be able to be alone, sir." The doctor's expression turned serious.

"Well, ain't got nobody at home."

"Then we'll have to see about a nursing home or some other facility."

The old man began to protest.

Mandy interrupted him. "You'll come to our house."

The doctor shut the chart with a snap. "Good. I'll be back later to check on you."

Mr. Shonee turned to Mandy. "I ain't disruptin' your lives. I'll be fine at home."

"That's ridiculous. You heard the doctor. You're staying with us. You can have our son's old room on the first floor. It's right by the bathroom. And you're not going to argue."

"Stubborn woman." He groused and looked away.

"Stubborn old man." Mandy laughed. "I'm going to go get Jon so he can see you. Don't go anywhere." She winked.

"Funny," he muttered.

৶৵

Jon pushed aside the curtain. "Hello, Mr. Shonee. I hear you're going to stay with us for a while."

"I don't reckon that wife of yours takes no for an answer very well."

"That's true. She can be pretty stubborn."

"Say Jon..." He pulled the mask away from his mouth. "I...I want to thank you for helping me. I hear I wouldn't be here if you hadn't found me."

Jon reached to replace the mask. "No problem. Just glad we were driving by. Jenny's the one who saw you out there."

"That young girl Kane was holdin'?"

"Yep."

"Guess I owe her some thanks, too."

"I'll pass that on. We all want you to get well now, but you'll need to do what the doctors say, you know. This is serious. We'll keep watch over your place while you're here."

"Why do you suppose the good Lord spared me like this, Jon?"

"I don't know, Mr. Shonee. But I'm sure glad he did."

Mandy came through the curtain. "Hi. The nurse said I could come back, now."

"You two need to get on out of here. You got better things to do than sit here starin' at me in a bed."

"We're not going anywhere until we know you're OK."

"Bah. I reckon they'll take good enough care of me here."

The nurse walked in. "OK, time's up. He needs to get some rest now. You can come back later."

"But..." Mandy started.

"If I have to listen to her, so do you," Mr. Shonee growled. "I'm fine. You go on home."

Mandy sighed. "All right, but I'm coming back later to check on you."

"Good. Do that. Now get out of here. I want a nap."

Mandy placed a kiss on the old man's forehead.

He grinned beneath the plastic mask.

Jon led Mandy out of the room and draped his arm over her shoulders. "Let's get home and make some dinner. We'll come back tonight before visiting hours are over."

"Oh, my gosh. I have a whole meal in the slow cooker. He was supposed to come for dinner tonight."

"Now my mouth is watering. Come on. Let's head out, and then eat."

26

Back at the ranch, they let everyone know Mr. Shonee was doing well. Sighs of relief followed plans for various pursuits, now that the tension was dispelled.

"Hey, Jon, can I speak with you for a few minutes after dinner?" Rick asked.

"Sure, meet me at the pond in about forty-five minutes."

Mandy and Jon went home and Mandy got dinner on the table. After the blessing they ate in silence.

"You OK, honey?" Jon broke into her thoughts.

"Yeah, I am," Mandy said. "Just worried. I hope Mr. Shonee doesn't have any lasting effects. Don't you find it strange how well he's doing?"

"Well, yeah, but look how much prayer covered him. We were right there when it hit. We may never know why, but we can really be thankful. This day could have ended much worse."

Jon helped Mandy clean up the dishes then went out the door.

Rick sat on the bench at the far end of the pond. The water reflected the trees above him and lazy clouds were drifting by. He was staring at the water.

"Hey, Rick."

"Oh, hi, Jon. Hey, thanks for coming out. I just wanted to talk to you a bit. I won't keep you long."

Jon sat on the bench. "No problem, what's up?"

Rick picked a tall blade of grass and peeled it

apart, tossing the green strips into the water.

"Rick? What's wrong?" Jon put a hand on the other man's shoulder.

"I've been thinking about what happened to Mr. Shonee today. Frankly, everything that's been happening lately."

"It's been a bit overwhelming, hasn't it?"

"That's an understatement. I thought I'd lost my little girl. Twice! Thankfully, we got her back. Then Mr. Shonee should have died, but he didn't."

"So...what are your conclusions?"

Rick leaned against the wood slats, stretching an arm across the back of the bench. "I'm not sure, but I do know you guys prayed a lot in both cases." Rick stared across the pond as if looking for something from long ago. "I lost my dad about five years ago."

"Oh, I'm sorry."

"Yeah, he had a heart attack too, but he didn't make it. He wasn't anywhere near Mr. Shonee's age. It's hard to understand. Do you think all that praying you guys did had anything to do with it?"

"Yes, I do. We believe very strongly in prayer, but that doesn't mean your dad died because no one prayed."

"That's what I wondered. We weren't a praying family, so after seeing what happened today, it made me wonder."

"Do you have any faith, Rick?"

"No, not in God. Never saw the need. Never saw a reality of Him...until today."

"And what did today show you?"

"You know as well as I do that the odds of that man coming through this heart attack were slim, at best. Just the CPR alone on an old guy like that could

Sandy Nadeau

have cracked ribs and punctured a lung. I heard Mandy praying right away, and when Nate showed up, you all prayed. Why?"

"Well, several reasons. First of all, as a believer, God wants us to pray. To take all our concerns and fears to Jesus. We trust Him to help us get through difficult times. We also believe that Jesus is the True Physician, the healer of all. Sometimes those prayers go the way we want them to, sometimes they don't. We can't understand the mind of God, but we can be obedient to Him. We also pray for the comfort that prayer gives us. We didn't want to lose Mr. Shonee, so we prayed, asking God to spare his life. I'm glad it went that way this time."

"It's very interesting. I'm not sure I understand it. Jenny seems very curious about God right now after going to church."

"How do you feel about that?"

"I don't know. But if it helps her feel better, then it's good."

"You know...Nate and I try to meet every Tuesday night to study the Bible together. Since you're going to be here all summer, do you want to join us?"

"I don't know. I might. We'll see."

"Think about it. We'd love to have you. Guy's night, ya know. We need that, too."

"Yeah, I'll think about it. Remind me."

"Will do."

"So, what's going on up at the mine site?"

"You know, with everything that happened today, I have no idea. I guess I ought to walk on up there and see what got done today. Want to go with me?"

"Yeah, let's go."

They made their way around the pond and

headed for the service road to the mine.

❧

Mandy stepped out on the porch when the men came from the pond. "Hi guys." she waved.

"Hey," they said in unison.

"I'm heading into town to check on Mr. Shonee one more time. I've only got about an hour, but maybe I can talk with the doctor again."

"Do you want me to go with you, Babe?"

"Oh, no. That's OK. I'll be fine. I should be home around 8:30 or 9:00."

"You know…Jenny needed some things from the store. I told her I'd take her to town in the morning. Could she just go with you now?"

"Oh, sure. I'll go tell her I'm going. See you later."

"Drive carefully." Jon kissed her cheek. "We're just going to go up by the mine and see what got done today."

"Oh, good. Have fun."

The men were nearly up the service road when Mandy and Jenny went by.

Mandy waved as she pulled out of the property.

Jenny waved, too.

❧

At the hospital, Mandy had only a few minutes to visit with her very groggy neighbor. She said a prayer, kissed his forehead, and left the room. "Can I see his doctor to ask about progress?" Mandy asked the nurse at the station. The woman nodded and directed her to wait in the lobby.

Jenny was already seated there, waiting for Mandy.

The doctor came through the swinging doors. "We're going to get him moved up to the cardiac unit as soon as a bed becomes available. He's remained stable and slept most of the time since arriving, but we want to keep a very close eye on him for the next 24 hours, which are crucial. He's scheduled to have an angioplasty tomorrow afternoon to clear the artery, provided his situation doesn't worsen." The doctor scratched his head. "It's the most unusual case I've seen for a man that age to come through this well."

"I'm not too surprised. We covered him in a lot of prayer from the time we found him, to arriving here at the hospital. He has a whole church praying for him."

"Well, that could explain it. I've seen prayer do amazing things beyond my training in the past. I guess God is still working."

"That He is. That He is. Thank you, doctor, for all you are doing. I appreciate you taking the time to talk with me. I'll be back in the morning to see him. He's not in much pain is he?"

"No, the medications will help him get some rest. He had much worse pain lying out in his yard before you found him."

"OK. Thanks for speaking with me," Mandy said.

The doctor nodded and went back through the doors.

The sun set beyond the hills as twilight moved in.

"Well, let's get to the store and head back to the ranch. I need more milk, so I'm glad you needed to come. It's nice to have the company. I'm whupped, though. I'll sleep well tonight. I hope."

"Me, too. I hope you don't mind stopping."

"Oh, that's fine. Like I said, I need milk anyway."

⊰∘⊱

The van headed down the highway taking Kane and Mark to a larger, more secure county jail facility.

Kane's teeth gritted so hard, his jaw began to ache.

Mark and that woman ruined everything.

His old man had a heart attack and was in the hospital. If he died, Kane would inherit everything, including the money the old man squirreled away. There were no other family members. It was rightfully his. Wasn't it?

Looking at the back of Mark's head fed his anger. He struggled against the hard plastic tie that bound his hands together.

Mark turned at the constant movement.

"What are you lookin' at?" Kane snarled out.

"Nothin'." Mark faced forward.

"Jerk." Kane thrust his bound hands into the back of Mark's head.

"Ow!" Mark shouted as the seat belt held him from escaping another blow.

"Knock it off back there," the deputy yelled from the driver's seat.

Kane hit Mark again.

"Kane, quit it. Leave me alone."

"What's the matter, girlie boy? Can't take it?" He hit him again.

Mark tried to duck out of the way but Kane persisted.

Kane released his seat belt, rose up, and began pummeling Mark.

The driver veered from side to side on the road

yelling for them to settle down.

Kane continued his attack. He could finally take care of Mark.

The young deputy yelled at them, and then looked back through the black grate that separated the front from the back.

Out of control, the van swerved.

෧ஂ஬ఀ

Mandy and Jenny headed back to the ranch.

Twilight had turned to night.

Up ahead, Mandy saw headlights moving from side to side on the roadway.

"What's that guy doing up there?" Jenny asked.

"I don't know, but I'm getting out of his way." Mandy turned onto a side road, and then turned the car to face the main road. "What's wrong with that driver? Is he drunk?"

The van over-corrected, hit the edge of the pavement, and then rolled into the ditch. Metal flew in every direction. Dust, dirt, and grass flew from the ditch as the vehicle tore a deep gouge into the earth.

Mandy's headlights illuminated the entire horrific scene. She threw the shift lever into park and screamed, "Oh, my gosh. Jenny, get my cell phone out and call 911."

A shocked Jenny tore through the contents of Mandy's purse trying to find the phone.

Mandy ran across the road.

The van had come to rest on the passenger side. Smoke and dust continued to fly around the severely damaged vehicle.

She had to try to help whoever may still be alive

inside the van. Her breaths were short, and her heart pounded. She made her way down into the steep ditch.

"Be careful," Jenny yelled.

Someone pulled themselves out of the broken side window.

"Are you all right?" Mandy crept closer. "Be careful."

The tall man dropped to the ground. His form was silhouetted by the light from her car, and she couldn't see his face.

"Are you hurt? Is anyone else inside the van?" she asked.

"Well, well…"

That voice stirred great fear in her soul.

"…Fancy meetin' you here." He grabbed her arm.

Mandy screamed and tried to pull away.

27

Half past nine already.

Jon looked out the window expecting to see headlights turn into the driveway any minute. The street light illuminated their large *High Country Safaris* sign. He'd called the hospital and the desk clerk said Mandy had left with Jenny sometime before.

"Well, Barney, where is she? I'm beat. I want to go to bed."

The dog lay on his pillow near the fireplace. He whined quietly, and then plopped his head down.

"You're a big help." Jon sat in his recliner and began to read. Soon the book drooped to his lap; he fought to stay awake. Sleep won as his head rested against the cushioned back of the chair.

ॐ

Jenny heard Mandy scream.

A tall man was pulling Mandy….a tall man…Kane.

Mandy was fighting with him.

Jenny fumbled with the phone, frantically trying to get it out of the case and turned on. "Come on, come on," She whispered as the phone went through it's starting up phase.

"Jenny, run. Get out of here," Mandy screamed.

The phone beeped and Jenny dialed 911.

"What's your emergency?" a woman spoke.

Kane reached in through the open driver's door and tried to grab the phone while still holding Mandy's arm in a death grip.

"Give me that," he growled.

Jenny leaned against her door, raised her feet up and began kicking at the man. Frustrated, she realized the seat belt restricted her ability to turn enough to kick harder. Jenny tried to get unbuckled, but her hands wouldn't cooperate.

"What's your emergency?" the voice on the phone kept repeating.

"We need help!" Jenny's foot made direct contact with Kane's face. "We're being kidnapped by Kane Shonee!" Jenny yelled, hoping the operator would hear her as she kicked.

A trickle of blood ran out of his nose. He swung his free hand at her knocking the phone to the floor.

Mandy continued pummeling his back with her free arm.

Kane grabbed the phone and threw it out the door as he backed his upper body out of the car. Then he opened the driver's door and threw Mandy into the front seat with one fluid motion. He reached into the pocket of his orange jump suit and pulled out a gun. "Both of you stop screaming right now."

འ∽ འ

They both froze.

Mandy sent a silent plea for help to God. *"Please God, Jenny's so young…help us…"*

"Now shut up!" Kane slammed the driver's door shut and got in the backseat. "Now ladies, we're going to get out of here together. You drive," he pointed the gun at Mandy. "But I'm going to have this gun pointed right at this lovely young lady, so if you try anything, that bullet will go through her head before you can blink. Understand?"

"Kane, just take the car. Leave us here."

"No. Shut up and drive. I'm going to need you. Head to the left. Take that first road to the south. Now."

She started the car and put it in gear, silently praying for the Lord's protection. She tried to reach over to comfort Jenny, but Kane yelled at her to keep her hands on the wheel.

❧

Barney barked loudly which woke Jon from his slumber.

"Is she home, bud?" He stood, groggy from the nap. He looked at the clock on the mantel. He'd been asleep for an hour. Mandy should've been back by now.

He rubbed the back of his neck, blinking away the sleep. He opened the front door fully expecting the two girls to be there laughing about something, but instead the sheriff stepped up on the porch.

Rick and Connie were rushing across the parking area.

"Hey Ed," Jon's heart rate increased. "What's up? Do you know where Mandy and Jenny are?"

"I think we need to sit down inside, Jon."

Connie went into a panic. "What's happened? Where are they? Is Jenny hurt?"

Ed ushered them inside. He took off his hat, but remained standing. "Mark and Kane were being transported tonight to the main jail. The transport van got in an accident out on county road twelve. The deputy and Mark were badly injured and were still in the vehicle. Kane's gone."

"What's that got to do with Mandy and Jenny?" Dread poured into Jon's heart.

"Dispatch got a frantic 911 call. There was just a lot of screaming for help. We found the phone on the road near the accident. It's Mandy's phone, Jon."

Jon jumped up, followed by Rick.

Connie fell into the couch crying. "What are you saying? Does Kane have them again?"

Rick's hands pressed his temples. "This can't be happening! Where are they?"

"We don't know." The sheriff spoke solemnly. "We've got every available officer out looking and we called the surrounding counties to be on the lookout for them. We know what kind of car to look for, so that will help." Ed walked over to Jon and put his hand on his shoulder. "We'll find them Jon, we'll find them."

"Yeah, but will you find them in time…?"

28

"Pull in here," Kane demanded.

Mandy turned the car onto the secluded lane. Towering pines lined the sides. Nothing but complete, total darkness lay beyond her headlights and off to the sides. Her brain worked in high gear trying to figure out how she could get them out of this situation without getting hurt.

Jenny hadn't spoken a word since Kane pointed the gun at them. The dashboard lights glowed against her ashen face. Tears ran down her cheeks, but she made no sound.

"Down there," he waved the gun in the direction he wanted Mandy to go.

The narrow road headed down a small hill. There were a few empty cabins on each side of the road. The headlights lit up the final darkened cabin at the end of a driveway.

Mandy put the car in park as she looked in every direction. No sign of life, no lights, not even any traffic sounds. What was she going to do? She could not subject Jenny to any further terror from this man. She killed the engine. "What are you going to do with us, Kane? Do you know your father is in the hospital right now?"

"Yeah, I heard. Don't care. I just want my money. Get out of the car. You slide out this side." He pointed to Jenny.

Mandy opened her door.

Kane waved the gun between the two of them.

The only light came from the stars up above.

"You got all the money off the sale of the rhodochrosite you stole off our property." Mandy spoke. "What more do you want?"

"That was rightfully mine. I found it years ago. We owned that property."

"Not after your dad sold it." Mandy got so angry she couldn't hold her tongue.

"Shut up. Get in there." He pointed to the rustic cabin.

The old wood door gave easily when he kicked it in. Thankfully, the cabin had power. He hit a switch as they entered which lit a small lamp in the corner.

Jenny held Mandy's arm in a death grip.

"Get over there and sit down." He pointed to an old dusty sofa with wooden arms.

"What are you going to do now, Kane? You'll never get away with this and you know it." Mandy said, as she and Jenny sat down.

Kane dug through the drawers in the small kitchenette that was part of the same room. From the bottom larger drawer he pulled out some clothesline rope. He threw it at Mandy. "Tie the girl to the arm."

Jenny put her hands on the arm, eyes wide with fear.

Mandy gave her a reassuring smile even though she had no idea how they were going to get out of this. She tied the clothesline around Jenny's arms and the wood, making sure it wasn't too tight.

Kane waved the gun for her to sit on the other side of the sofa.

Mandy scooted over.

He knelt down near the end, grabbed her wrists in

one hand and laid the gun on the floor. He held them tight against the wood as he took up another piece of the rope.

She could kick him but she didn't have enough strength to overpower him. With Jenny tied, she couldn't make a run for freedom. Maybe she could kick him enough to knock him over and grab the gun. Her fear of Jenny getting hurt in the process was too great. *I need another plan, Lord…*

Kane moved to Jenny and checked her knots, and then he sat in a chair.

"Can you at least find us some blankets? It's cold in here."

Kane went into the adjoining room and came out with two blankets. He covered them and sat in the chair again.

"Well, now what are you going to do, Kane?" Her tone held a twinge of sarcasm.

He didn't respond. He only tapped the barrel of the gun against his leg.

Quiet filled the room. No sound came from outside.

Kane stretched out his long legs. He rested his head against the back of the chair and closed his eyes. The gun, still in his hand, lay in his lap. Soon, his snores filled the room.

Mandy tried to wriggle against the ropes, but it did no good.

Jenny curled her legs on the couch. She tried to mop away the tears with her shoulder. Then she rested her head against the back of the couch, sniffing.

"Just pray, Jenny. Just pray." Mandy leaned her head against the couch and prayed until she drifted off into an uneasy sleep.

Rick and Connie remained in the house with Jon.

"Where could they be? That man is crazy. What's he going to do with them?" Connie cried.

Jon stared out the window into the black night. "I don't think he'll hurt them. We have to believe that. He must just be using them to get away."

"But then what?" Rick demanded.

"I don't know."

"So, are your prayers going to do any good now, Jon?"

Jon looked him square in the eye. "Yes they are, Rick. I have no doubt. Prayer is all we've got for protecting them now, and I'm not about to give up on that. God will get us all through this. You can either believe that or give up."

"So why didn't your God protect them and keep them away from that man?"

"Don't argue, you guys! This is hard enough to deal with. I can't listen to that, too." Connie's voice was wobbly.

The men went silent.

Jon looked out the window saying even more prayers in his mind.

Rick sat next to his wife and put his arm around her.

Barney paced, picking up on the tension in the room.

Nothing more could be said. The night wore on.

Connie fell into a restless sleep leaning on Rick. Her muscles twitched in unsteady rhythm.

The two men just sat and stared at nothing.

৵৽

Mandy woke when light began to sneak through the window.

Jenny was asleep in an awkward position.

Kane remained stretched out in the chair.

She had to figure out a plan to get them out of here. She prayed in silence.

Jenny stirred. She tried moving, and then her eyes opened. She looked at Mandy.

"Good morning," Mandy mouthed the words, not wanting to wake Kane.

"I have to go to the bathroom," Jenny's voice came out in the tiniest whisper.

"Me, too."

Mandy wondered if she could get out a bathroom window and run for help. No, that wouldn't work. Jenny would be at his mercy. Maybe Jenny could escape and run for help. Mandy could take care of herself.

Kane yawned loudly, stretched, and looked over at the two captives. "Mornin', Sunshines." His voice dripped in sarcasm.

"We have to go to the bathroom, Kane." Mandy used as forceful of a voice as she dared.

"Too bad." He growled and walked out of the cabin. The slam of the door shook the small cabin's walls.

"Jenny, he's got to let us go to the bathroom sooner or later. When you go in, see if you can get out the window and run to find help."

"Where would I go?" Jenny's eyes were wide. "What if I get lost? He'll hurt you if I'm gone. I can't leave you with him. And what if he catches me out there?"

"Shh, shhhh…Listen, I know where we are. This is a group of cabins owned by the O'Neil family. They use them during hunting season. There is a lodge not far from here. If you can get back out to the main road, go to the right. It's a ways, but you can do it, Jenny."

"I don't want him to hurt you…" More tears fell.

The door burst open and Kane stood with a bag from the car. "Look what I found. You brought us food." He took the groceries to the kitchen.

A low humming noise sounded in the distance. A low-flying helicopter. The authorities were looking for them. It had to be Search and Rescue.

Kane darted out the door. He returned, demanding the car keys.

"You'll have to untie me so I can get them for you," Mandy said. "You better hurry though, or they're going to see the car."

Kane untied one of her hands.

She dug in her front pocket, and then reached into her back pocket.

"Come on!" He pointed the gun at her head.

"I'm trying…" She hoped she'd stalled long enough for the people in the copter to get a look. She brought out the keys.

He grabbed them and ran back out the door. He'd forgotten to re-tie her hand. The car started up, and she heard gravel being kicked up as he peeled out of the driveway. Mandy pulled frantically at the knot on her other hand. She leaned down, using her teeth to work the knot. Tears of frustration leaked onto her arm.

The door slammed open again. Kane came in, and his eyes opened wide with realization. "Don't even think about it." He re-tied her hand to the wooden arm. "Well, they aren't going to see us now. Yer stuck with me."

"And just what good will that do you? Do you think you can just keep us here indefinitely? Why don't you just take the car and leave?"

"Well now, that would be pretty stupid with them helicopters up there, don't ya think? No, we're going to hang out here for a while till I decide what we're going to do."

"Then let us go to the bathroom."

"Dang women. Fine."

He made a move towards Mandy. "No, let Jenny go first."

"Whatever." He began working on Jenny's knots, his back to Mandy.

"Go for it. Do it." Mandy silently mouthed the words to Jenny.

"I can't." Jenny mouthed back, her gaze pleading.

Kane pulled her to her feet. "Go do your business and come right back out. Don't try nothin' or she'll pay for it."

Jenny looked at Mandy and shook her head.

Mandy gave her a firm nod. *"Oh Lord, please give her the courage to get out the window and run. Please!"* Mandy stared at the door as if she could will the girl out the window.

A couple minutes went by.

Kane knocked on the door. "Hurry up, kid."

"Give her enough time, Kane. Gosh, it was a long night, you know."

"I don't care. Hurry up in there."

The door knob turned. Jenny walked out and sat on the sofa. Her expression was contrite. "I'm sorry," she mouthed to Mandy.

Kane's head was down as he re-tied Jenny. He missed their silent communication.

"It's OK," Mandy reassured the girl.

"You gotta go, too?" Kane looked at Mandy.

"Yes."

He untied her. "Don't try anything funny."

Mandy went to the bathroom and shut the door. She took care of things, and then reached up to look out the window. It was small, but Jenny would be able to fit.

"Hurry up!" Kane bellowed.

"I'll be right out." She turned the water on and looked out the window into the woods for a possible escape route. There wasn't enough underbrush to hide. She opened the door and couldn't miss the relieved expression on Jenny's face. She headed to the sofa.

"You go make us breakfast," Kane growled. "And just so you know, I hid all the knives so you can forget any dumb ideas. Just get us something to eat."

Mandy went over to the small kitchenette, opened the fridge and took out eggs and milk. In seconds, she was cooking and pondering if she could throw the hot mixture in his face.

But Kane kept his distance.

She opened the bread bag. A quick search in the lower cabinets, revealed a toaster. And on the inner side of that cabinet, there was a small pocket knife tucked behind the trim. She took the knife and slipped it into the pocket of her jeans. Somehow, she would find a way of escape. She stood and continued stirring the eggs, seasoning them with salt and pepper.

29

Jon rushed outside when Ed pulled into the driveway.

The Carters had gone back to their cabin for a quick shower and change, but they were already heading back to Jon's house when they saw the sheriff's car.

Hearing the car, most of Jon's employees gathered around, anxious for news.

"Any sign of them?" Rick asked.

"No, sorry. We're not giving up, though. We'll find them. He hasn't called with any demands has he?"

"No, nothing. There's been nothing." Jon rubbed his unshaven face, quelling the anxiety in his heart.

A collective murmur went through the crowd.

"We've had no reports from the surrounding counties of your vehicle, so we're thinking he's somewhere within our boundaries. He's holed up somewhere, waiting for a better time to escape. A lot of the cabins in the area haven't been opened yet for the summer season, so now we're searching those."

"OK, Ed. Thanks," Jon sat on the top step of their porch.

Barney made his way over and leaned against Jon's side. The dog was usually attached to Mandy. With her missing, the dog had not left Jon's side.

The sheriff left.

The Carters joined Jon on the steps and stared after the car.

Jon absentmindedly rubbed Barney's ear.

The ranch employees drifted away and went back to work.

Nate put his hand on Jon's shoulder. "You get any sleep last night?"

"Uh, no. Not much."

"Come on, all three of you." Nate motioned to the house. "You need something to eat. I'll fix it. Come inside."

"I can't eat." Rick's face reflected fear and anger. "I need to do something. I can't just sit here and wait any longer. We need to go look for them."

Nate turned to him. "Rick, I understand your frustration, but the sheriff has all his department out looking, even the helicopters. There's nothing more we can do."

"No Nate, I agree with Rick," Jon spoke. "We're going crazy sitting here doing nothing. We know the area better than anyone. We need to get out there."

Connie nodded her head, eyes pleading. "Please, anything for a solution to this awful waiting."

"All right," Nate relented. "But you'll have to eat while we plot out where we can go look."

Jon called Sue on his radio and asked her to get the topographical map.

Nate led the three into the house.

Sue brought the map and then took over coffee making duties, while Nate cooked eggs, bacon, and toast. He handed out plates piled with food.

Jon took a plate, bit into his toast, and laid the map out on the kitchen table. "Connie, I think you should stay here. I don't want you to end up in a dangerous situation if we do find them. We'll keep the radio on us so you can contact us in case the sheriff shows up with any news."

"I'll stay with you, Connie," Sue volunteered. "We'll be here in case they escape and manage to get home."

"All right, but you have to call in periodically so I don't go nuts waiting to hear from you." Connie gave Jon a hard glance.

"I promise we'll check in with you." Rick hugged his wife.

Connie leaned her head against his chest. "Find her, honey. Please bring her back to me."

As the men walked out the door, Jon turned back. "Sue, can you try and check on Mr. Shonee? I don't know how we're going to handle telling him what's going on now with Kane. See if you can talk to the doctor and tell him the situation. Maybe they can stall in explaining why we aren't coming in to visit."

"I'll take care of it, Jon. Don't worry." Sue headed for the phone. "You've got enough on your plate right now."

❧❦

Mandy dished up the eggs. "Are you going to untie her so she can eat?"

Kane sat in a chair against the side wall, the gun in his hand. "Nope. She'll have to figure out how to eat tied up."

"Come on, Kane. At least give her one hand. She can't eat like that."

Kane slammed his chair forward and stood. "I'm gettin' tired of your lip, lady." He loomed over Mandy in a threatening manner.

Jenny's eyes went wide, and she looked at Mandy.

"I can do it. That's OK."

"Put the plate on that table next to her," Kane demanded.

Mandy helped Jenny position herself. The ropes had just enough give to allow her hand to raise a short distance to her mouth if she slouched down.

"Now, you. Sit down." Kane re-tied Mandy's hands and thrust a plate at her. She had to eat off the plate just as Jenny did.

"Lord, bless this food we are about to eat and thank You for Your blessings. In Jesus's name I pray, amen." Mandy prayed out loud, and then began to eat.

Jenny bowed her head as soon as she heard the beginning of the prayer, but Kane continued to eat, ignoring them.

Mr. Shonee would be expecting them to visit. How would he feel if no one came in to check on him? She had to convince Jenny to make a run for it. She had to come up with a plan. She wondered if Kane had any sympathetic feeling for his father. She decided to take a chance. "Your father's lying in the hospital with no one around, or worse. What if his condition goes downhill?"

"I don't care." Kane spoke with his mouth full. "He never cared about me."

"You know that's not true. He just didn't like you taking advantage of him. He took care of you for a long time."

"Ha. That's a laugh. He never got off my back."

"He just wanted you to be responsible."

"Shut up! I ain't gonna talk about him no more."

Mandy and Jenny went back to being silent, and clumsily finished the food on their plates. Mandy finally gave up.

Kane took their plates, stomped into the kitchen, and threw them into the sink. "I'm goin' outside. Ya best be here when I get back." The door slammed.

Mandy squirmed so she could get the knife in her pocket.

Jenny's eyes went wide, panic filled her voice. "What are you doing?"

"I found a small knife. I'm going to cut our knots." She struggled against the ropes.

"Mandy…"

"Jenny, I have to do something to get us out of here."

"I'm scared of him. What if he hurts us?"

"I'll make sure he doesn't." Mandy managed to open the blade and began awkwardly sawing at the rope.

The door slammed open.

She closed the knife and hid it in her fist. "Will you stop slamming that door?" Mandy demanded.

Kane snorted and pulled a curtain aside to look out. He didn't see the knife in her hand.

☙◦❧

Nate drove the vehicle with Jon in the front seat, Rick in the back. They had decided the ranch's smallest vehicle, a two-door Jeep, would be fast and small enough in any tight and rough areas.

They headed out to where the sheriff found Mandy's phone.

Jon and Nate spread the map open, discussing possibilities.

"We need to check all these backwoods areas," Jon pointed to the green area of the map. "There's a ton of places that would still be empty since last fall. We must be overlooking the obvious. Let's drive off to the right and see if we spot anything."

Nate turned the Jeep onto the main road. He kept under the posted speed limit so they could look down side roads and pull over, if necessary.

They drove down driveways and old dirt roads but there was no sign anywhere.

෧෴෧

At the hospital, the nurses prepped Mr. Shonee for the angioplasty in the cardiac catheterization lab.

"Anybody come in to see me yet?"

"Not that I know of, Mr. Shonee. You really can't have visitors right now, anyway. The desk would have informed any visitors of that. They're probably in the waiting room, as anxious to see you as you are to see them. We'll take good care of you, not to worry."

"Kind of funny they aren't here. But maybe they got turned away."

The nurse patted his arm. "Didn't you say they run a tourist ranch or something?"

"Yeah. Some kind of four-wheelin' ranch."

"Well, maybe they had to organize other people to take care of their guests this morning and couldn't get here in time to see you before you came in here." She tried to ease his mind. "Don't you be nervous, now. We know what we're doing."

"I guess I'll have to trust ya." The old man winked at her.

The doctor came in and explained that they were going to send the catheter in through his arm. "All your tests came back and this will be the easiest on you. Once we are done, you'll need to be still for a while, but once everything seals up well, you'll start to recover fast. You'll probably be surprised how quickly you'll be feeling better; more so than you have for a while. So as we give you this medicine, just relax. We'll get this taken care of."

"All right, doc. I reckon I'll just lay here prayin' while you do your thing. I sure wish Mandy were here, though."

∂∞∾

Kane went into the other room and when he came out, he was dressed in plain clothes. They were a little large, but the belt cinched the pants tight. He tucked the gun in the belt against his back. "Well, ladies, according to your car radio, they're really lookin' for us. So what are we gonna do about this?"

"Why don't you just leave us here, take the car and make a run for it?" Mandy suggested.

"Maybe I'll just hold you for ransom. How much money you worth to that man of yours?" Then he looked at Jenny. "How about you? Yer parents pay much to have you back?"

Jenny couldn't look at him. She'd spent too many hours stuck in a dark cave with him, and now she was a prisoner again under his sneering looks. She hoped and prayed if she ever got out of this, that she would never have to see him again. Fear made her heart hammer so loud she was worried he'd hear it.

∂∞∾

Mandy could see the building fear in Jenny and

prayed for wisdom. "Kane, it isn't going to do you any good to get a ransom. Didn't you get enough out of the rhodochrosite? Can't you just settle for that and leave?"

"It wasn't enough." He stomped close to Mandy. "I had a great thing going until that girl stumbled in on our claim. It's your fault," he roared in Jenny's direction. "I could have had a lot more."

Jenny was shaking so hard the cushions on the sofa vibrated under Mandy. She realized too late that she needed to use a different tack to keep him off balance. "Why don't you check around outside to see if there's another place to hide and give you time to figure out what you're going to do?"

"I'm tired of listening to you, anyway." He slammed the door as he marched out.

"Are you OK, Jenny?"

"I'm so scared, Mandy. I don't want to be here anymore. I want to go home." Tears ran down the young girl's cheeks.

"I know, honey. We have to figure out what to do."

"I think I'm ready to make a run out the window. But, where do I go?"

"Are you sure?"

"Yeah, I just don't want him to hurt you."

"Don't worry about me. We have to get you out of here to get some help. You'll have to stay off the road that we came in on, so run through the woods as fast as you can. If you veer off at an angle to the right, I know you'll run into the property with the lodge on it. You just have to do your best to stay on a straight course in that direction." Mandy nodded her head, unable to point with her hands.

"What about wild animals though, Mandy? What will I do?"

"It's daylight hours, Jenny. You won't even see anything."

"Are you sure?"

"Yes. You can do this. Just get to the lodge and get help. Flag someone down if you have to."

"OK, Mandy. I'll do it. Please don't let him hurt you, though." Her pleading gaze broke Mandy's heart.

"I'll be fine," she whispered as she heard his footsteps coming up the steps outside.

Again, he burst through the door.

Mandy had prepared for it this time. "Jenny needs her bag out of the car, and then use the bathroom."

"Tough."

"Come on, Kane. She's a girl." She hoped Kane would get what she was implying.

He stood there for a moment glaring, and then went back out the door. She heard him slam the tailgate of her Jeep Cherokee and come back in with the bag. He tossed it on the sofa between them and went to untie Jenny's hands.

The girl cringed being so near him. Once her hands were free, she rubbed her wrists, looked at Mandy, grabbed her bag, and went into the bathroom.

Mandy struck up a conversation so he wouldn't hear Jenny open the window. She prayed in her mind even as she spoke. "Kane, seriously, we can't just stay here indefinitely. What if you just drove away? They're going to be looking for all three of us in a vehicle. You won't draw so much attention if you go alone."

"I haven't decided yet." He began to look through all the cupboards in the kitchenette. Owners knew mice would tear into anything left behind in a cabin over winter so they didn't leave much.

Mandy worked the knife against the ropes since his back was to her.

"There isn't enough food for us to stay here long, is there? You need to make a decision."

He slammed the cupboard doors, then walked over and slumped down into the chair.

"Just make a run for it in the car. Leave us here so we don't slow you down. You know the area. You can get out of here. Head for the old mill road. You could make your way out over the trails in that direction. My car can handle it."

"Will you quit talkin'? Geez, woman. Shut up for a while. What's takin' that girl so long?"

"Leave her be. She has to take care of things."

Silence.

Mandy kept her gaze on the man and prayed for the Lord to guide Jenny to safety. She prayed for wisdom, strength, and courage. Her heart pounded. She shook deep inside, and her palms began to sweat.

Kane cocked his head to the side listening for Jenny in the other room. When he realized there was no sound in there, he jumped up and pounded on the bathroom door. "Answer me, girl!" he yelled. "What are you doing in there?"

"Kane..." Mandy tried to distract him.

He ignored her and continued pounding.

She kept cutting at the ropes on her wrists.

Kane backed up and kicked at the door, slamming it open. He looked inside and must have seen the window open. He turned, cussed, and ran for the door.

Mandy's ropes came free. She stuck out her leg and braced herself.

He tripped over her shin and flew face first into

the hard wood door. He staggered, holding his head.

Mandy gathered every bit of courage she had and sailed, shoulder first, into his mid-section. She knocked him off balance and caused him to fall backward.

His head made direct contact with the small table next to the chair he had slept in. He went limp and didn't move. The man was breathing, but he was unconscious.

Mandy got the rope, rolled him on his side, and grabbed the gun from his waistband. She tossed it over to the sofa and tied his hands and feet to the sofa.

She picked up the gun and flew out the door. "Jenny." Running towards her Jeep, she hollered again, "Jenny!" She hopped in, set the gun on the floor of the passenger's side, but the key wasn't in the ignition. She frantically searched the floor and checked the visor. It had to be in his pocket. She groaned and ran back to the cabin. Cautiously, she opened the door.

He was still out cold. A red bump rose on the center of his forehead, and his nose bled.

She rummaged through his pockets, found the keys, and ran back out the door.

"Jenny!" she screamed. "Jenny, I got away!"

No one replied.

The Jeep started right up. Mandy slammed it into gear and pushed the gas pedal all the way to the floor. The tires spun in the dirt, kicking up rocks.

"Oh Lord, please. Show me where Jenny is, and help me get out of here." Mandy scanned the woods anticipating where Jenny might run. Nothing. She honked the horn several times hoping Jenny would hear it. The Jeep bounced on the ruts in the dirt lane as she drove for all she was worth.

❧❧

Jenny dropped out of the window scratching her left leg as she slid down. She landed with a muffled thud and froze. Not hearing anything, she took off running.

She ran in the direction where he wouldn't see her if he looked out the window. Again, she found herself running through the uneven, slippery, dry pine needles of a Colorado forest. Fearful of falling into another hole, she dodged around bushes and kept to open ground. "God, I need you, again. More than ever." She gasped the words out as she ran. "Please help me find someone. Please keep Mandy safe." Tears blurred her vision as she ran. Jenny ran for her life, and that of her friend.

30

Mandy saw the main road up ahead. She slid to a stop at the end of the lane. No traffic. She peeled out onto the pavement. She had to find Jenny. She slowed, keeping a closer eye on the woods. Where could that child be? If she ran, she should be near the road by now. She looked in her rear view mirror and saw another car approaching. She veered onto the shoulder to let the car pass. Did they know her? They drove past oblivious to her dilemma. Another one approached so she waited for it to pass.

❧❧

Nate squinted and leaned over the top of the steering wheel. "Jon, isn't that Mandy's car?"

Jon looked up from the map, put his hand on the dash and yelled, "Pull over, pull over. That's Mandy."

The Jeep slid on the dirt shoulder behind the Cherokee.

Jon was out of the vehicle before Nate brought it to a complete stop.

Nate whipped out his phone to call 911.

❧❧

Mandy watched in her mirror as the car screeched to a stop behind her. Fear gripped her at first, but then she saw Jon. She opened the door and ran back towards him.

"Mandy. Dear Lord. Are you all right?" They slammed into each other.

Tears and deep sobs poured out of Mandy.

Jon held her and ran his hand over her hair on the back of her head.

"Where's Jenny?" Rick's voice cracked with emotion.

"She got away. She has to be out there," she pointed to the woods. "I told her to run in this direction. Kane had us in the O'Neil's cabins. He's tied up down there. We have to find her, I've been calling and calling but I haven't seen her or heard her."

Sirens echoed in the canyon heading in their direction.

"Jenny!" Rick called as he scrambled into the ditch to get in the woods.

Jon called to him. "Let's get back in the vehicles to search for her. There's a road up ahead we can turn in and look."

"I told her to head for the lodge."

"Nate, you and Rick head for the lodge, we'll take the road down into the woods in case she hasn't gotten that far yet."

"Right." Rick and Nate hopped back into the Jeep.

Jon looked over at his wife as they buckled up. "Are you all right?"

"I'm fine, now. Oh Jon, she was so afraid. We have to find her. I convinced her to escape out the bathroom window and go find help." Mandy started crying again. "She has to be safe."

"How did you get away?"

"I found a small knife when he made me cook breakfast. By the time he realized Jenny was gone, I had managed to cut through my ropes, so I tripped him. Then I pushed him and he got knocked out."

"That's my girl." Jon smiled and cocked his head. "Don't worry, Mandy. We'll find Jenny and this will be all over with."

The helicopter was overhead. It flew over the surrounding forest.

Someone was bound to spot Jenny.

∂∾∾

"Help me, Jesus," Jenny cried as she ran around trees and hopped over small bushes and rocks. Her strength was giving out. She came to a stop, panting, and leaned hands on her knees to catch her breath. She looked in every direction for any sign of humans. She took off running again.

Then she heard the helicopter. They wouldn't be able to see her with the dense tree tops. She searched for any opening in the pine canopy above. She ran back and forth hoping that they would see her through the trees. The copter flew directly overhead.

Jenny waved her arms and screamed.

The chopper vanished. Silence filled the forest.

Jenny fell to the ground on her knees, gasping for breath, and cried. "Help me, Jesus. Please? I need help. I'm scared."

I am with you.

Puzzled, she looked up. Tears streamed down her face.

Trust in Me. Do not fear.

"Lord?"

Suddenly a feeling of great peace filled her entire being as if arms of warmth and comfort enveloped her.

The tears continued to run down her cheeks, but she felt safe. She raised her head and dried her tears on her sleeve.

Was that a road? She stood and started to run. Then she saw it.

Mandy's Cherokee.

Was it Kane?

"Oh, my gosh!" She watched as it approached, trying to stay hidden by the girth of the ponderosa pine.

There were two people in the car. Relief flooded Jenny's soul when she saw that Jon was driving and Mandy sat in the passenger's seat.

Jenny ran out into the open screaming for them.

❧❦

"Jon, stop!" Mandy screamed. She unclipped her seat belt and almost fell out the door. Running, she caught Jenny up into a bear hug, clutching the girl like she'd never let go.

"Mandy, you're safe. How did you get away?" Jenny held on to her tight, shaking, crying, and breathless.

Jon put his hand on Jenny's shoulder and held out a phone. "You need to say hi to someone."

Mandy released her hold on the girl.

Jenny took the phone and said through her tears, "Dad? Oh, Dad! Yeah, I'm here with Mandy and Jon. OK. See you in a minute. Hurry, Daddy." She handed the phone back to Jon and flung her arms around Mandy again. "Are you really here?"

Relief filled Mandy's heart and she thanked God, but she couldn't answer through the tears.

The helicopter hovered over them. Jon gave a thumbs up signal. The pilot waved back, understanding. The chopper banked and flew away.

Jon put his arm on Mandy's shoulder. "Let's head back out towards the main road.

"How *did* you get away?" Jenny asked in the car as she wiped at her tear streaked face.

Mandy had her arm hanging between the bucket seats to hold hands with the girl.

Jon laughed. "She knocked him out!"

"What?"

"I finally cut through my ropes as Kane tried to figure out why you wouldn't answer the bathroom door. When he ran for the front door to go after you, I sort of...tripped him." She gave Jenny a rueful grin. "He fell into the door, but then he backed up holding his head. I knew I better do something fast so I jumped up and slammed my shoulder into his belly. He fell backward and hit his head on the table so hard it knocked him out."

"Where was the gun? Why didn't he try to shoot you?"

Mandy grinned, reached down and picked up the gun. "You mean this?"

"How did you manage that?"

Jon had a huge smile on his face while he drove. "He apparently didn't have time to get it while he was getting beat up by a girl."

They all laughed.

31

Nate and Rick met them on the road.

Rick grabbed his daughter and enveloped her into his arms, squeezing her so tight that Jenny protested.

"Dad, I need to breathe."

He let her go, unashamed of the tears running down his face. He kept stroking her hair, and took her hand as if he never wanted to let her go.

Mandy understood exactly how he felt.

The sheriff also pulled up. "Well, ladies. I can't tell you how happy we are to see you alive and unharmed." He paused for a moment, blinking his eyes. And then he hugged Mandy, released her, and patted Jenny's shoulder. "We were right scared for you two." He looked down, brushed unnecessary wrinkles in his uniform, and then turned professional. "I need to talk with both of you. The police are on the way to the cabin to capture Kane."

"I have the gun he used." Mandy told him. "It's in the Jeep."

"I'll take that, then." Ed accompanied her over to the vehicle and pulled out a plastic evidence bag. After he took it, he waved to the men, got in his car, and headed to the cabin.

"Rick, Jenny, Mandy, why don't you all come with me," Jon suggested. "Nate needs to be on hand if the sheriff needs anyone to do traffic control, if word gets out and the lookie-loos show up. No doubt the media will be here soon."

They took off for the ranch.

Connie tried to open the door before Jon could even stop the car. Jenny fell into her mother's arms, both of them clinging and sobbing as they greeted one another.

Rick wrapped his arms around both of them. The family stood there for a long time holding on to each other and allowing the emotions to bubble over.

Sue came out of the house and hugged Mandy. "It sure is good to see you, my friend."

Barney hopped around, trying to get in on the hug action with his favorite people, Jenny and Mandy. He finally went over to Mandy and leaned against her leg.

Nate drove up, letting Jon know his services weren't needed by the sheriff.

A crowd of employees, as well as a few guests, gathered in the parking lot.

When Mandy and Jenny turned to face everyone, a huge cheer went up. Everyone wanted to hug them or talk about the relief of finding them. Knowing they needed closure, Mandy spoke with them all. Jenny held up like a trooper, talking gently with the children who were in awe of her harrowing escape.

Finally, as the crowd dispersed, the cook came over. "I'm going to bring over a bunch of food so you can all eat in peace."

"Thanks, Alice. We'd appreciate it." Mandy turned to the Carters. "Come on. We have a lot to talk about. Nate, Sue, why don't you join us, too?"

"What on earth happened? I want details." Connie demanded.

Mandy explained the accident they witnessed on the way home from the store and how she ran over to help, only to find Kane crawling out.

"That must have been horrifying." Connie wrapped her arm tighter around her daughter.

"Oh, Mom, I was so scared." Jenny laid her head on her mom's shoulder and continued, "He's so mean. He kept us tied up in that cabin. We couldn't even go to the bathroom unless he let us. Then he made Mandy cook and we had to eat while tied up. I was so scared that Mandy would get hurt. When she found that knife, I thought if he found out, he would shoot her, or both of us."

"We did a lot of praying, I'll tell you that," Mandy murmured.

"I don't think praying did you any good," Rick said. "Look what you had to go through. Why would God allow such a thing to happen to two innocent people?"

"Rick, it's times like this that I depend even more on Jesus to get me through."

"Yeah, Dad. You know, when I ran through the forest trying to find help, I got so tired and scared. I didn't know what was happening to Mandy. I kept thinking Kane would be coming up behind me. When I stopped to catch my breath, I broke down and cried out for Jesus to help me, and when I thought I wouldn't be able to go on, the weirdest feeling came over me. I even thought I heard a voice telling me to trust Him. It was weird, but then I felt so much better. When I looked up, there were Jon and Mandy. I'm sure that God brought them to me."

"Well, I don't understand why God would put you through it all in the first place. So what if He helps you through something? Why can't He stop it in the first place?"

"Rick, God loves us all so much that He gave us a

free will to do as we want," Nate explained. "If He forced everyone to believe in Him, to do the right thing all the time, then we wouldn't be choosing a life with Him. We wouldn't have any need for Him if everything went great in our lives. He doesn't want us to come to him by force. He wants us to see that we need Him in our lives. Kane exercised his free will by doing dreadful things to innocent people. God still watched over Mandy and Jenny. God won't force Kane to do the right thing. Kane would have to choose to give up the evil heart he's built up over the years."

"But why?" Rick asked. "He made the wrong choices. Why would God allow my daughter to suffer through so much torment from the hands of that man?"

Jon responded, "We may never know, Rick, but God uses all things to bring about a good result for those who love Him. He knows what will happen. He knows what we can handle. He made His presence known to Jenny out there in the woods. He held on to her and helped her."

Mandy picked up her Bible off the side table and turned to Psalm 73:23-26. "'Yet I am always with you; you hold me by my right hand. You guide me with your counsel, and afterward you will take me into glory. Whom have I in heaven but you? And earth has nothing I desire besides you. My flesh and my heart may fail, but God is the strength of my heart and my portion forever.' God will always be faithful to us as believers."

"Well, I don't get it. I just don't. This has been too much to go through for there to be a God."

Alice and another kitchen helper came through the back door with trays full of food. "Come and eat everyone," she called out.

Nate walked over to Rick. "We'll do what we can to help you understand, Rick. But some things we just won't ever understand."

"I'm just glad they're home safe," Rick said as he walked into the kitchen with everyone.

While they were eating, two squad cars pulled in to the ranch, red lights flashing.

Jon rushed to the door. They all stepped out onto the porch as Sheriff Ed walked up. Another deputy got out of his car, stood near it, and looked around the area.

"Ed?" Jon's voice held great trepidation. "What's going on, now?"

The sheriff removed his hat. "We went down to the O'Neil's cabin to pick up Kane. He's gone."

Connie, Jenny, and Mandy gasped and covered their mouths with their hands.

"The door was wide open. There were ropes scattered on the floor, but no sign of Kane. We found blood, but not much. We called in the dog teams to head out in the woods to search the area. We're going to keep the helicopters up for a while longer, as well. For now, I think you all better stay inside and together. I'm posting a deputy outside."

Nate stepped around everyone on the porch. "I'm going to gather the guys. We'll guard all the way around the house."

"I don't think he'd dare come back here, but I do think you should warn your guests, and maybe keep them in camp until we find him. We're also going to post a guard at the hospital." Ed was solemn. "After what you told us Mandy, about his feelings for his dad, we need to keep an eye on him, too."

"I'll get on the radio and call the guests back in." Nate spoke into his radio.

Connie pulled her daughter into the house. "Is this never going to end?"

Mandy put her arms out to gather everyone. "We'll just hang out together today. They'll find him. I know they will."

Rick's face and neck reddened. "I'm starting to rethink the idea of staying on here. Rhodochrosite or not, this is not worth my family's lives."

"Dad..." Jenny whined.

Jon interrupted. "Rick, let's just wait this out. They'll find Kane and things will settle down. We need to just stay put for now until he is caught."

"At least he doesn't have a gun anymore." Jenny tried to lighten the mood.

"He doesn't need a gun to cause more trouble." Jon said as he checked the doors and windows to be sure the locks were secure.

❧∞❧

Mandy paced the room as she worried about two very different men. She called the hospital and waited for a call back from the doctor as to Mr. Shonee's condition. "I'm no good at waiting. I want to go see him. He has to feel hurt that we haven't come in to see him at all today. Here he's having that procedure done, and no one is there to support him."

Jon leaned forward in his recliner. "I know honey, but we can't take a chance on leaving right now. Not until that man is found and locked up."

Connie sat on the couch, quiet, her concern evident by her expression. Jenny petted Barney, who rolled over and laid his head against her, but when she noticed her mom, she joined her on the couch. "You OK, Mom?" Jenny asked while rubbing her hand on her mom's back.

"Yeah, I'm OK, sweetie. I just keep thinking about everything you went through out there and it scares me."

Rick stood silently and stared out the window.

Jenny reached her arm around her mom's back. "I don't think I've ever had so much happen to me at one time before. Wait till all my friends hear about this trip."

"How can you even think about it?"

"Well...it's over now, Mom. I've found out how much it helped me to pray to get through it all. I don't know. It just makes me feel better. Now that I'm safe, I think back on it all and I can see how God protected me."

"I wish I could feel as secure as you do about this."

Mandy sat on Connie's other side. "It's always harder as a mommy to find peace when your child is in danger. Remember that verse I read? He is my peace. I have to take comfort in Him."

"But how do you find peace like that?" Connie held out her hands. "I used to go to church, but we just...fell away, I guess."

"You just have to believe in Jesus, Mom. Now I finally understand what they all meant at church. When you have nothing else, when it's all gone, when there's nothing around to depend on, you still have Jesus to see you through. It's cool! He's like the best friend you could ever have."

"Oh honey, I wish I could understand what you mean."

Jon leaned back. "We don't have much else to do, would you like to do a little Bible study to pass the time?"

"Yeah, let's do that." Jenny's enthusiasm bubbled over.

"How about you, Rick? I'd like to help you understand Who God is."

"I don't care." His words were clipped. "Connie and Jenny want to hear it, so go ahead. Like you said, there isn't much else we can do right now." He remained stoically staring out the window.

Jon got his Bible off the sofa's end table. He went back to his chair and opened the well-worn book to the first chapter of John. "This is the chapter that really helps you understand who Jesus is. Why God had to send Him for us." He began to read. "'In the beginning was the Word, and the Word was with God, and the Word was God. He was with God in the beginning. Through Him, all things were made; without Him nothing was made that has been made. In Him was life, and that life was the light of men. The light shines in the darkness, but the darkness has not understood it.'" Jon went on to read about John the Baptist coming ahead of the One. He explained that even though Jesus was in the world, people didn't recognize Him as God. "'The Word became flesh and made His dwelling among us. We have seen His glory, the glory of the One and Only, who came from the Father, full of grace and truth.'"

"But what does that all mean?" Connie's face seemed puzzled.

Jon looked over at her. "Jesus is the creator. He created all things. He was there from the very start, and even though He came from God as a man to live with man, He was still fully God. Because of His love for us, that's why He came to be with us. Kane made it obvious; the heart of man can be sinful. God cannot be around sin. It required a sacrifice. Jesus came to be the Lamb for us. Listen to chapter three. 'I tell you the truth,' Jesus said, 'no one can see the kingdom of God unless he is born again.'" Jon then stated from memory, "'For God so loved the world that He gave His only Son, that whoever believes in Him shall not perish but have eternal life.'"

"We just have to believe that, Mom, then He's in your heart forever."

"I heard a lot of this as a child growing up, but I never knew what it meant." Connie had a faraway look in her eyes.

Rick finally turned around, acknowledging that he'd been listening. "It has to be harder than that. If God is really God, it can't be a simple thing."

"But that's the beauty of it, Rick." Mandy looked over at him. "It's simple for us, but it wasn't for Christ. He gave His life on the cross for us all. He suffered for all the sin of all mankind for all time. You said earlier that this has just been too much to go through. A lot of people go through much worse things. Families suffer through cancer, losing a child to death, rebellion that breaks their hearts...any number of things happen to many people. Life isn't easy for anyone, but if you have Jesus in your heart, you have Someone to turn to. Someone to bring comfort when you don't know where else to turn. And you get eternal life in heaven on top of it."

Connie turned to Mandy with pleading eyes. "So how do I get this?"

"The Bible says that everyone who calls upon the

name of the Lord will be saved. You just have to believe that God sent Jesus, and that He died on the cross for our sin. He rose from the grave and now sits at the right hand of God. His Holy Spirit is here with each one of us to comfort us."

"But I don't understand it all."

Jon's smile brightened his face. "That's OK, Connie. Jesus just wants your heart first, the learning takes a lifetime."

"Rick?" Connie turned around to look at her husband. "What do you think?"

"Yeah, well, it all sounds good, but I still have my doubts. It just can't be that simple."

"Daddy, I just think you'd be a lot happier if you had Jesus for a friend. I want us all to end up in heaven."

Rick walked over to his daughter and hugged her. "I know honey. I think it's wonderful that you have found this to believe in."

"But, what about you, Dad? Do you believe it?"

"I'm just trying to understand it all right now, sweetheart."

The phone rang.

"Yes..." Mandy said into the receiver. "I'm so glad you called. How is he doing?"

They all waited, listening to her side of the conversation.

"OK, I'm glad it went well...yes, we have had more trouble with his son and we're not able to come right now...no, I don't think he should be told....I agree...can I call him later? Good, OK, thank you, Doctor. Goodbye."

She looked at everyone. "They did the angioplasty on Mr. Shonee this morning. The doctor is very amazed at how well he is coming through all of this. Because of the procedure, they don't think he should know about Kane, yet. They told him he couldn't have company yet, so when they find Kane, we'll go visit him. But he's doing well."

"Praise God." Jon looked up.

"Hmm..." Rick said.

"What?" Jon asked.

"Well, it's still pretty amazing how well that old guy is doing. How could he have made it through?"

Jon smiled. "Something to think about, isn't it Rick?"

32

The sheriff pulled into the parking lot of High Country Safaris. Everyone met him at the door with hopeful expressions.

Nate ran up from the barn.

"We got him." The sheriff punched the air to accentuate his words.

"Where'd you find him?"

"Well," the sheriff began, "apparently, Mandy, you pack quite a wallop. He passed out and lay dazed at the bottom of a ravine only about a half mile from the cabin. The dogs found him. My guys got down there and apprehended him, and he still didn't know what was going on."

"Oh, my gosh." Mandy's hand flew to her mouth. "I didn't think I pushed him that hard. Is he going to be OK?"

"It serves him right to be hurt." Rick growled out his anger. "Don't be concerned about him, not after what he did to you and Jenny."

Mandy looked to Rick. Her brow pinched. "He's just a lost man, Rick. He's Mr. Shonee's son."

"Well, anyway..." Clearing his throat, the sheriff continued. "He'll get checked out at the hospital, and then he'll be locked up tight for a very long time. He's got a long list of charges against him."

Jon slapped his hand on their friend's shoulder. "Thanks, Ed. Maybe now we can get things back to normal around here."

"Yep, I hope so. I wanted to let you know right away. He isn't going to get away this time. Take it easy. I'm heading for the hospital. I have a few things to say to that guy. See you later."

Everyone said goodbye to the officer and thanked him.

Jenny jumped up and down with a squeal, then spun a circle.

Rick took Connie's hand. "Come on. We're going to the cabin."

Confusion filled Connie's face.

Jenny wore a frown as she headed after her parents.

Nate looked at Jon. "I think we should do something special tonight for all the guests after calling them in today. Seems we need some damage control for the Carters, too."

"He is really hardened towards God. I don't want them to leave before we can reach him." Jon stared after the family.

Nate gripped Jon's shoulder. "I know buddy. We have to trust God to take care of him. It's up to the Holy Spirit, now."

"We need to get to the hospital and see Mr. Shonee," Mandy reminded. "Let's have a campfire tonight. We could have Alice make up some steaks to cook out there for everyone. Let's have a party."

"Aren't you exhausted?" Jon turned to his wife.

"Not any more. There's just too much to celebrate to be tired right now."

Nate went to the door. "You guys go on. I'll talk to Alice and let the guests know. We'll have a big ol' hoe down tonight!"

࿒࿒

Jon and Mandy walked into Mr. Shonee's room.

His bed was elevated and his face lit up as they entered. "Well, hey there. I didn't think you'd come see me today."

"Sorry we couldn't be with you, earlier," Jon said. "Things came up that we had to attend to."

"You look so much better." Mandy's tone warmed. "How are you feeling?"

"Not too bad. A might frustrating earlier to lie still while things healed up, but I hear they got me all fixed. Should be good as new."

"Well, you sure have been covered in prayer." Jon shook the man's hand.

"Doc keeps tellin' me he can't believe I made it through all this. Not quite sure myself, except for that prayin' you been doin'. I uh…well, I don't suppose I thanked you two enough for comin' along and savin' me and all."

Mandy sat on the edge of his bed and took his hand. "God did the saving, in more ways than one. God used our words and our hands to accomplish what He wanted done. I'm so glad you're going to be all right."

Jon made his way around the bed. "And you are going to come back to our house when they release you. No arguments. We want to take care of you."

"I've got it all figured out. You can stay in our son's old room. It's right there on the first floor by the kitchen so you won't have any stairs and there's a bathroom next to it. I'll cook you some healthy meals and make sure you recover completely. We'll check on your house too, and make sure everything is all right over there."

"Oh tarnation…all this fuss. You two are more stubborn than me."

Jon laughed. "You won't be able to win against Mandy when it comes to taking care of someone. So count on being our guest for a while. She's the most stubborn."

"And don't you forget it." Mandy gave a mock ferocious glare.

They all laughed. They visited for about half an hour before a nurse came in and said he should get some rest before dinner.

"We'll be back tomorrow." Mandy promised as she kissed the top of Mr. Shonee's head and patted his shoulder in good-bye.

The old man actually blushed, sputtered a good-bye and waved them out.

❧☙

As the car pulled into the driveway, Jon and Mandy spotted Jenny sitting on a large rock at the end of the first row of cabins. Barney leaned against the rock as she rubbed his head. Jon parked the car and they walked over to the girl.

"What's up, sweetie?" Mandy asked.

Jenny sighed, but kept her gaze on Barney. "Dad says we're going home."

"I'm sorry to hear that," Jon said.

"I don't want to go home. I was all excited to stay here all summer. It's not fair."

"I know you're disappointed honey, but your dad has to do what he thinks is right," Mandy said. "He's just worried about you. He loves you."

"Well, Mom doesn't want to go, I don't want to go and if he loves us he would let us stay."

"When are you leaving?"

"In the morning." Jenny's lower lip stuck out.

"Maybe you can come back some time." Tears escaped from Mandy's eyes. "I'm really glad we got to know you. Well, it wouldn't have been my first choice on some of the time we spent together…"

Jenny finally looked up and grinned. "That's for sure. I'm glad I got to know you, too. I'm sure going to miss you, though. You're the only one who talks to me without treating me like a child." Jenny hugged Mandy.

"Well." Jon stood, hoping to lighten the mood. "For now, we'll just have a great time at the campfire tonight. Tomorrow will take care of itself."

Mandy sniffed and finally let go of the girl, wiping away the tears. "That's right. We're going to have a great time and celebrate that everything worked out. We have a friendship that will last forever." She patted Jenny's shoulder. "We have to get to work so we can have the campfire tonight. Will you be OK?"

"Yeah. But I'm really going to miss it around here." Jenny gulped down tears. "I'll miss you too, Barney." She rubbed the top of his head, and the dog leaned against her.

33

Evening rolled around and everyone started coming down to the campfire area.

Mandy's heart warmed at the sight.

Alice flipped steaks on a large iron grate over one side of the fire. Piles of foil-wrapped potatoes lay within an oval of very hot rocks near the flames.

Phil and George tuned up their guitars. There were six families gathered, and even the two fishermen who'd had the mountain lion experience. They already reported to everyone that their friend was doing much better, and could go home in a few days, although he was talking about finishing up his fishing trip.

Mandy called the church to invite more people. Families drove into the parking lot and joined in on the fun, including Pastor Bob and his wife.

Dean went and sat by Jenny.

Connie was all smiles.

Rick sat unemotional.

When the steaks were ready, Jon asked Pastor Bob to bless the food.

Pastor Bob looked around the circle of people and spoke up. "If you would, join me in prayer." He bowed his head.

Everyone followed his lead, except Rick.

"Lord, we have so much to be thankful for tonight. Mostly for the safe return of Jenny and Mandy. Lord, we know that only through You were they protected and brought back to us safely. We thank You for the arrest of the individual responsible for all the difficult circumstances of late. We do pray for that man's salvation Father, that he will somehow turn his life over to You and repent for all he has done wrong. Lord, we know we are all guilty of sin and able to cause heartache and we just ask that You forgive us as we try to live better lives. We ask that You watch over our brother Al Shonee and bring him home soon. Now Lord, we ask that You bless this wonderful meal. We thank You for the hands that have prepared this food. And please lead our fellowship tonight. In Jesus's name, we pray. And all God's people said…"

"Amen!" The reply echoed from everyone around the fire pit.

A table off to the side held plates, silverware, and side dishes. The kids pushed their way into line first. The lighthearted mood filled the air and soon everyone settled in with their food around the fire.

One gentleman asked of Jon, "So how is the little town site coming?"

Nate jumped in to answer. "All the foundations are in and the framing crew started today constructing the structures. It'll take a couple of weeks to rough it in, but we are on the right track up there."

Sue sat down next to Mandy with her food. "The professor from the Colorado School of Mines called this afternoon and said they would be coming out tomorrow to scope out what needed to be done on the Jackson Mine to shore it up. They are very excited to get the students involved with it."

"I'm so glad everything seems to be coming together now." Mandy placed a hand to her heart.

The plucking of a guitar started and soon the two ranch hands were comically entertaining with their brand of campfire songs.

❦

Jenny sat next to Dean. She couldn't think of a thing to talk about. She moved the food around on her plate with her fork, barely eating any of it.

Dean leaned over and focused. "Don't you like our potluck?"

"Huh? Oh, no it's fine. I guess I'm just tired or something." Jenny couldn't even look at him.

"I know you're sad about leaving, Jenny. Maybe your dad will bring you back, sometime. I'm glad we got to become friends."

"Me, too. I don't want to leave. I wanted to spend the summer here. I wanted to come back to your Sunday school class. I wanted to have some more fun times to make up for what Kane took away from me. I had just started to learn to ride horses. It just isn't fair." She set her plate on the ground in front of her.

"I know. But hey, we have some great stories to tell." Dean smiled in a way that lightened up her mood.

Jenny finally giggled. "I don't think my friends back home will believe it."

❦

Pastor Bob refilled his plate for another helping of the salads and a couple of the double chocolate brownies, then headed over to Rick and Connie. "Mind if I join you?" He stood next to the log bench they sat on. The fire crackled and snapped.

Connie smiled. "No, please. Join us."

"I always have liked these get-togethers around the fire pit at the High Country Safari ranch. These people know how to throw a party."

"They do seem to have fun, despite everything that has happened." Connie tried to continue the conversation since her husband wasn't participating in it.

"Are you two doing OK after everything that has gone on? Our church sure prayed hard for all these difficult circumstances that have gone on. I'm sure glad Jenny is OK."

"Well...we're leaving in the morning," Connie said quietly.

"Oh, I thought you were staying on for the summer. Rick, weren't you going to do more exploration of the cave on the west side of the property?"

"How could I possibly keep my family here after all that has happened to our daughter?"

"Oh, I can understand that. As men, we have a great need to protect our family. I commend you for that. But, surely you realize that the threat is over..." Pastor Bob said.

"All I know is that the past two weeks were supposed to be vacation, but have turned into one heart-wrenching experience after another."

"We did have some fun times..." Connie tried.

"From what I understand, there have been a lot of instances where God's protection was very evident."

"Again with God!" Rick spat out. "Where was God when that beast took Jenny captive in a mine? Where was God when he took her again with Mandy? God hasn't done any favors around here." Rick tossed his plate down on the bench and stomped away.

Connie watched her husband walk towards the pond. "I'm sorry, Reverend. He's been very upset by everything."

"Oh, I understand. Do you think I could go talk to him?"

"I'm not sure if he'll listen, but you're welcome to try."

The pastor put the last bite of brownie into his mouth, set down his plate, and walked after Rick. The music filled the air along with laughter from the group.

⤙⤙⤚⤚

Jon had his arm around Mandy's shoulder and Mandy had her arm around Jon's waist.

The fire crackled, lighting up everyone's smiling faces. Some of the kids lined up to roast their marshmallows for s'mores, the traditional camp cookies made with graham crackers, melted chocolate, and hot, squishie marshmallows.

Barney roamed around watching for any food tossed aside.

Phil started playing an old Irving Berlin song, stretching out the first word so the older generation had time to pick up on the words and join in. Soon the kids were mimicking the adults and the chorus continued. Everyone laughed as George took on the next verse.

Jon sighed and whispered in his wife's ear, "Ahh...this is more like it. This is how life is supposed to be."

"So you don't want any more excitement?"

"No, I don't. I don't ever want to experience the possibility of losing you ever again."

"I'll second that. It's time for a boring summer, now."

"We'll see if that happens." Jon gave a rueful grin. "It could be challenging to have Mr. Shonee here. He's pretty set in his ways."

"I think I can handle him."

☙❧

Morning came and Mandy found Jenny down at the corral. Barney stood at her side. The songbirds filled the air with their music. As Mandy walked up, she could hear sniffles coming from the girl. "Hey, sweetie. Good morning. Checking out the horses?"

Jenny had tears running down her face. She threw her arms around Mandy's neck. "Oh, Mandy...I don't want to go home."

"Oh, honey, I know, but you have to go by your dad's decision. Who can blame him? You've been through so much the past couple of weeks."

"I don't care. It's all over with now. I know he wanted to dig deeper into the rhodochrosite mine. Why would he leave that?" She cried harder.

"Because he loves you very much." Mandy smoothed Jenny's hair as she held her. "He wants to protect you from any more bad things."

"Bad things can happen at home, too. We should just stay here."

"His priority is you, Jenny. You can always return. Maybe after things get back to normal for a while, he'll want to come here again."

"Maybe," the girl sniffed. "I'm just going to miss you and Jon and especially Barney so much."

"We'll be right here waiting for you. We can

always e-mail each other..." Mandy led her to a bench near the corral. They sat down and quietly watched the horses meandering around the corral.

Mandy teared up. She pulled a tissue from her back pocket and handed one to Jenny.

∂∘∾

Jenny realized how much she would miss the ranch. Barney had been her buddy the whole time. He stayed with her when she thought she was alone. She found Jesus was her friend and He would be with her no matter what. She made friends at a church. She really liked Dean. He was so cute. She recalled the rides up into the trails surrounding the ranch. She remembered the sharp gray, snowy mountaintops. How fast the storm rolled in over the mountains. The elk, the deer, the white fuzzy babies and the pine trees. Everywhere they went, there was so much more to see. She loved it here. She preferred it to the crowded neighborhood she lived in.

She'd started out mad at her folks for making her leave her friends. Now, here she sat crying and mad at them again that she had to leave. She sobbed into Mandy's shoulder.

The sun made it up over the hill to the east. The birds chirped and flitted around at the feeder by the house. The jays squawked loudly up in the trees.

Mandy and Jenny just sat there quietly taking it all in together.

"Hey, you two."

Jenny turned, tears still streaming down her face.

Mandy did her best to hold back her own tears.

"What's with all the crying around here?" Rick

asked.

Jenny sniffed, wiping at her eyes. "I don't want to go, Dad. I want to stay here."

"Is that why you're crying?"

"Y-yes."

Rick stood near the bench next to Jenny. "I've been talking to your mom."

Sniff.

"We decided we're going to stay." Rick smiled.

"What? Are you kidding?"

"I'm not kidding."

Jenny flew off the bench and flung her arms around her dad, almost knocking him over. "Oh, Dad. Thank you. I'm so excited." She hugged Mandy, and then ran off yelling for her mom. Barney was close on her heels.

❧❦

Rick watched her go, and then turned to his hostess.

Mandy patted the bench, indicating he should sit down. "What made you change your mind?"

Rick sighed and sat down next to her. "You have a persuasive pastor."

"Well, that's true. But how did he persuade you?"

"He challenged me to at least take some time to get to know who God really is before I bail out and run. I didn't much like to hear someone say I was bailing out. I'm not one to give up, so I decided during a sleepless night that I needed to find out what it is that keeps all of you so devoted to God. Jenny seems so self-assured from her knowledge of God, and I thought she'd be traumatized. I'm sure she'll have issues, but she loves it here, despite what happened. Besides, that rhodochrosite keeps calling my name." He grinned.

Jon walked out of the office.

Mandy waved him over.

"Hey. What's up? You all ready to leave?" He looked to Rick.

Mandy and Rick grinned as they looked at each other.

"What?" Jon asked with a furrowed brow.

"Can I tell him?" Mandy asked.

"Sure, go ahead!" Rick smiled.

"Tell me what?"

"The Carters will be staying with us this summer, after all."

Jon extended his hand, which Rick took in his own. "I'm glad to hear it, Rick. Things will be better now, I'm sure of it."

"Thanks, Jon. Yeah, I think I need to stick around here and learn some things. And there are too many possibilities with that mine of yours to let it sit idly holding any more treasure." He looked over his shoulder as his wife and daughter came to join them. "I think this will be the summer to remember for my family. We've gotten closer. We've made it through some impossible circumstances, yet through it all, I think I've discovered that my time with my family is way more important than a job. If we are here, we'll be able to spend more time together as a family instead of me running off to another jobsite."

Connie smiled as she put her arm around her husband.

"Connie, I'm so glad you'll be here with us," Mandy said.

"Me, too. I think it will be good for all of us to

spend some more time here. Hopefully, a bit less dramatic in the weeks to come." She hooked a finger under her daughter's chin.

Everyone laughed and agreed.

Barney began a low growl. When the growl picked up in volume, it caught Jenny's attention. "What is it boy?" She knelt down.

He kept his gaze to the west and continued to growl.

The group looked up in that direction.

Smoke!

Jon began to bark orders to ring the alarm as he ran to the barn.

Mandy took off for the porch to clang the triangle that hung from the roof.

Ranch hands streamed out of the bunk house pulling on their boots. More came from the barn and garage. They hopped into the trucks with the gear, including the water truck, and took off out the driveway.

Mandy ran inside and grabbed the phone.

Rick sighed, followed Jon to the barn, grabbed a shovel and hopped into the Jeep with his host. "Yep, it's going to be a nice, quiet summer!"